THIS TIME AROUND

by
Chantal Fernando

CHANTAL FERNANDO

Published January 2014

Cover design © Ari at Cover It! Designs
Editing by Hot Tree Editing

This Time Around is a work of fiction. All names, characters, places and events portrayed in this book either are from the authors' imaginations or are used fictitiously. Any similarity to real persons, living or dead, establishments, events, or locations is purely coincidental and not intended by the authors.

Trademarks: This book identifies product names and services known to be trademarks, registered trademarks, or service marks of their respective holders. The author acknowledges the trademarked status in this work of fiction. The publication and use of these trademarks is not authorized, associated with, or sponsored by the trademark owners.

ISBN: 1495281477

ISBN-13: 977-1495281471

DEDICATION

For Akeirah.
In our arms for a little while, in our hearts forever.
Love you always, angel.

ACKNOWLEDGEMENTS

As always, I'd like to thank **Ari** from Cover It Designs for her amazing work, her advice and her friendship. Thank you for putting up with me! You are the best. No, really.

Thank you to my beta readers- **Kara Brown, Stephanie Knowles, Aileen Day and Claudia Juarez**. I am so grateful for your help.

Thank you to **Pepper Winters**, who is an amazing friend and always there when I need to chat or vent ☺

Thank you to **Becky at Hot Tree Editing**!

Thank you to all the blogs that promote me, I appreciate everything you do!

And of course to my readers… I can't explain how it makes me feel when I get messages from you all, telling me how much you loved my books.

There are no words.

I love each and every one of you.

Thank you so much and I hope you love Ryan as much as I do!

THIS TIME AROUND

PROLOGUE

Taiya

After all he's put me through…

I stomp my foot and grit my teeth. I didn't think returning to Perth would be like this. I didn't think I'd run into Ryan only a few days after my return, but I did. Lucky me.

I push off my car where I've been standing for the last ten minutes, parked in front of Ryan's bar. Knox Tavern. The place looks different since the last time I saw it. I walk in and my eyes immediately zoom in on him. I don't see anyone else in that room except him. I ignore the way my heart races at just the sight of him, the way my body responds. I storm towards him, needing to give him a piece of my mind. How dare he see me for the first time in a year, and ignore me.

He took one look at me, surprise etched all over his face. I saw a myriad of emotions flash before he concealed them and noticed someone standing next to me. Scott is just a friend of mine, and Ryan had no right to lay a hand on him. Ryan has no right to me at all anymore. He lost that privilege.

If only someone would tell my heart that…

But sorry, heart, my head is winning this one.

CHANTAL FERNANDO

CHAPTER ONE

Ryan

When she walks in, I'm surprised. No, I'm shocked. I never thought I'd see the day that she walked back into this bar, but here she is. Her curly brown hair frames her round face, and her blazing green eyes are narrowed in anger. Even angry, she is the most beautiful woman I've ever been in the presence of. My gaze can't help but wander down her shapely body. She's stacked in all the right places, and I should know, I've tasted every inch of her body many times over. She steps in front of me and purses her lips.

"You had no right, Ryan," she seethes, her voice low and shaking.

"I had every right," I reply calmly, trying to pretend this woman has no effect on me. When in truth, she owns me, body and soul.

Only she doesn't know it.

"I'm not yours anymore," she says, her voice losing its edge. She sounds resigned, tired. I don't like it one bit. I prefer her anger.

"You will always be mine," I say with a shrug.

"Ryan, I'm serious. You can't do this to me," she says with a shake of her head.

I lean in a little closer so I can smell her familiar scent. "Tell him to leave you alone then, Taiya."

"So you get to fuck anything with a skirt, but a good man can't even look my way?" she asks, gritting her teeth.

"Yeah, that pretty much sums it up."

I wasn't expecting the slap. But I should have. Taiya always did have a fiery temper on her.

"Fuck you, Ryan. Stay out of my life," she spits out before storming off.

I watch her walk away from me.

My wife.

I should be used to it by now, but it still hurts.

It always hurts.

*****

Thump.

Thump.

Thump.

And this is why I'm moving out.

A moan pierces the air, and I cringe, not wanting to hear Summer's cries of pleasure. Summer is like a sister to me, and to hear her making sounds like that… with my twin brother, let's just say there are a million places I'd rather be right now. I put my iPod on, blocking out their sex sounds. Summer and Reid didn't want me to move out, but I know for a fact that they need their privacy. So we compromised. I'm moving to another apartment. It's on the floor below, but on the opposite side of the building. That way, I can still see them every day, but we each get our own space and privacy. As unlikely as it is, I got the apartment with Taiya in mind. The image of her brings up mixed emotions.

Love.

Desire.

Want.

Pain.

I try to ignore the last one, but whenever Taiya comes to mind, the lingering emotion is always present. She is the only woman in the world with the power to hurt me, and that's exactly what she did.

Even if it wasn't her fault, or her intention, she did it nonetheless. I shove my face into my pillow, trying to block out how it felt seeing her again after all this time.

A year.

I hadn't laid eyes on my own damn wife in a year. I'm a fuck up. I know it; she knows it. But that doesn't make me stop wanting her. I don't think *anything* could make me stop wanting and loving Taiya. Maybe that's my penance for my past mistakes. I can actually hear Reid talking in my head, telling me not to think like that, nothing was my fault. Although I can hear the words, it doesn't mean they penetrate, or that I actually believe them. Nothing he says could make me believe them. I try to bury those thoughts, letting the music lull me to sleep.

*****

"I love it, Ryan!" Summer states, looking around. She is wearing a huge smile, her brown hair falling like a curtain around her face. I watch as she sits down on my new leather couch and shifts to get comfortable.

"Make yourself at home," I tease, shaking my head at her as she puts her bare feet up. She's wearing shorts and a ratty looking T-shirt, which looks like an old one of Reid's. Or it could even be one of mine.

She shrugs at me. "My home, yours, what's the difference?" she says flippantly, reaching for the remote and putting on the TV. She speaks the truth. My home *is* her home, and vice versa. Her phone beeps and I know it must be Reid. He is so whipped it's not even funny. I give him shit about it sometimes, but we all know I'm thrilled for the two of them. Reid couldn't have dreamed up a better woman, and I'm happy that he found her.

Summer changes the channel and then starts singing along to some ridiculous song.

"When's Reid done?" I ask, sitting on the chair next to her.

"He usually works out for an hour after work," she says.

"I know," I reply. I know my twin's habits better than my own.

"Should be home in about two hours then," she answers.

Summer drums her fingers along her thigh, in beat with the music. I lift my foot up on the arm of the couch, where the back of her head is, and put my toe in her hair.

"Ryan!" she yells, sitting up and narrowing her eyes at me. She picks up my new cushion and throws it at my head. I dodge it, but only just.

"What?" I ask. I love annoying this girl. She's like a sister and best friend combined into one.

"You're so immature," she says, no bite in her tone. She turns back to the TV, her hair flying everywhere as she turns her head.

"Never claimed maturity," I instantly reply. We've had this same conversation many times over.

A new song plays and she actually squeals. "This is my favourite song right now!"

"What is it?" I ask, slightly curious.

"'Gangsta' by Kat Dahlia," she says, putting the song full volume and ignoring me. When she starts rapping, I start laughing so hard my sides start to hurt. She is such a weirdo. I instantly recognise the song as the one she has as her ring tone. When it finishes, she presses the mute button and turns to face me. "You gonna tell me what's been up with you lately?" she says with the lift of an eyebrow.

"What do you mean?" I say, wanting to buy myself some time.

"You've been acting…off for the last two weeks. If this is about you moving, I told you I didn't want you to leave," she says, frowning.

"It's not that. You remember the woman who came into the bar and slapped me?"

"Yes, I've been asking Reid who she is but he keeps telling me it's your story to tell," she grumbles, crossing her arms over her chest.

I clear my throat. "She is my ex…" I trail off.

7

"I gathered that much," Summer says dryly. She moves so she's kneeling on the couch, facing me.

"We broke up. She moved away, and now she's back," I tell her. I'm leaving a fair bit out, but I don't think I'm ready to talk about what happened. That would make it real, and I don't want to see the disappointment in Summer's eyes when she finds out the truth. I still see the look on Taiya's face and it cuts me, right down to my soul.

"And you still love her," she says, her voice soft with understanding.

"I'll always love her," I tell her, looking away.

"What's the problem then? You're an amazing guy. She would be lucky to have you," Summer says, her voice hardening.

"She left on bad terms, and by now, she has definitely moved on," I say quickly. Even the words hurt. It's not my place, and I haven't been a saint while she's been gone, but that doesn't mean that it doesn't hurt. Emotions aren't always logical. I used different women to try and forget Taiya; it never worked and I'm not proud of it, but it's what I've done for the past year. Taiya's words in the letter she left behind told me to move on, and believe me; I tried. I'm never disrespectful to women, or treat them badly or anything like that. All the women I've been with know the score, and I'm still on good terms with them…except Taiya. I keep asking myself what is truly worse. Me having only physical relationships with different women, or her making an emotional one with a new man? I know there is no right or wrong in my situation, or if there were, I would be in the wrong. It's not that I don't want her happy either, because I want nothing more than that. It's just...I know no other man will love Taiya the way I do, know her the way I do. I don't regret punching her new boyfriend either. I hate to admit it, but it actually felt pretty damn good. To think he's had his hands all over her...

"Ryan, stop wallowing. If you want her, go and get her," Summer says, pulling me out of my thoughts. She glances down at my now clenched fists and grins. "I can see why she has you tied up in knots. She's possibly the most beautiful chick I've ever seen."

"She's a lot more than that," I say quietly, casting my gaze down.

"Do you want me to beat her up?" Summer says with mock ferocity, making me grin.

"No, I don't want you to beat up Taiya. But thanks for the offer," I tell her, shaking my head back and forth, amused at her words.

"What? I could take her!" she says, standing up and flexing her arms as proof.

"No one is *taking* anyone," I say. Summer bursts out laughing. "Try telling Reid that. Trust me, he will want to take me later," she says, her mouth lifting in a wide smile.

I cringe. "You worry me, Summer."

"You love me."

"I'm stuck with you."

"Yes, you are," she says, her voice going soft. "Listen to me. You are Ryan Knox. Local heartthrob and all-round amazing guy. Whatever you messed up, you can fix it. The question is how much work are you willing to put in to win her back? Just how important is she to you?"

I puff out a breath. "She's everything."

"There's your answer then," she says, looking a little smug.

"That easy, huh?"

"That easy," she repeats. I watch as she steps toward me, and leans down to peck me on the cheek.

"I gotta head out. Family dinner," she says, patting me once on the head like a dog before walking out of my apartment. The second I hear the door close, the place feels colder.

Summer has that effect.

My mind drifts to Taiya, to the last time I saw her. Besides her hair being a little longer, she is exactly the same as I remember her. Caramel-coloured skin, showing off her mixed South African heritage, intelligent green eyes and the most kissable lips. Don't even get me started on her body, but for me, Taiya is more than her appearance. She's smart, witty, kind and loving. She is as loyal as they come, and a woman that any man would be proud to have by his side. I had all that, and I lost it.

I hope to God it's true that everyone deserves a second chance.

CHAPTER TWO

"Hello Ryan, long time no see," Rita says in an accented voice. She flashes me a grin, and smooths her dark greying hair back off her dark-skinned cheek. "Come on in," she says, gesturing with her hand for me to enter.

"As always, you're a lot more welcoming than your daughter," I joke as she pulls me in for a quick hug, before I pass her. We both walk into the kitchen.

"Don't you start, Ryan Knox," she says in a mock stern voice.

I raise my hands. "Just stating the facts, Rita. Is Taiya in?"

"No she's not. And you used to call me mum," she says, her smile fading. I notice that she's lost a lot of weight, and looks tired.

"And if things go my way, I will be calling you that again soon," I tell her with a wink.

She doesn't smile like I thought she would. Instead, she says, "Taiya told me she gave you the divorce papers."

"She did. Everything was done, all I had to do was sign them and hand them over to my lawyer," I say, swallowing hard.

She nods her head twice before pinning me with her dark eyes. "I don't know how you're gonna fix this, Ryan."

I don't know how I'm going to fix it either, but I'm sure as hell going to try. "Where is she?" I ask, changing the subject. I really don't want to upset Taiya's mother, drilling her with questions about her daughter. I have about a hundred I'd like to ask, but instead I pick a safe topic.

"She's gone apartment hunting."

I nod. Of course, she would want her own place now that she's back. "How are you?" I ask, worried about the change in her appearance.

"I'm okay. Don't you worry about me," she says, grinning. "I think you have your hands full already."

I smirk, knowing how true that really is. "Nice seeing you again, Rita."

"You too, Ryan. You sure you don't want to stay for something to eat?" she asks, her gaze roaming over my frame, trying to see if I've lost weight. The woman is always trying to fatten me up.

"I'm fine, but thank you," I tell her. I kiss her on the cheek, before returning to my car, and heading straight to the bar. Knox's Tavern, AKA my second home, is completely dead with only one car in the car park. That car belongs to Tag. I walk in and see him standing there against the bar, checking something on his phone.

"Working hard, or hardly working?" I ask in a dry tone as I walk up towards him. He glances up and grins, before returning his attention back to the phone.

"I'm pretty busy, as you can see," he says, pointing to the empty, spotless bar. He slides his phone into his jeans and looks back up at me, running his finger through his goatee.

"You can head home early if you want," I offer, knowing he would love to have the extra time with his daughter.

"You sure?" he asks, slapping me on my back.

"Yeah, I think I can handle the excitement all alone."

Tag chuckles, "I'm sure you can. I'll see you tomorrow then."

"See ya, buddy," I say, taking out some of the paperwork I have to get done tonight.

Thinking that this was going to be a boring uneventful night, it all changes an hour later when Taiya herself walks into the bar. Tight jeans and top, my gaze can't help but roam a little south.

"Eyes up here, Ryan," she says, pursing her pink lips.

"That's twice in a week you've dropped by, Taiya. You miss me?" I ask. My voice is teasing but laced with hope. A man can dream, right?

"Yeah, like a disease. My lawyer just rang and said you didn't sign the papers," she says, crossing her arms over her chest. I try not to glance down at her breasts but fail.

"That is correct, yes." I didn't sign them, and I don't intend on signing them. That piece of paper is the last thing holding us together, our last tie. No way in hell I'm going to sever it. I'm going to hold on for as long as I can.

"You said you would take care of it," she says accusingly.

I sigh and turn to the fridge behind me, reaching down to pull out her favourite soft drink. I place it in front of her, and then continue the conversation, "I lied."

"Yes, you seem to make a habit of that, don't you, Ryan?" she says with a scoff, pushing away the drink with her hand, rejecting my peace offering. She taps her glittery nails on the table, her eyes... daring me. To say what? I have no idea what's going on in that head of hers right now, but I intend to find out. I used to know what she's thinking, know her better than herself, but right now, she has me stumped. I'm looking forward to getting to know her all over again, inside and out. I can't keep my eyes off her. I think I could stare at her for hours, noticing subtle changes since I last saw her. Smiling at things that are exactly the same. My eyes are hungry for the sight of her.

Wanting something so badly, having it right in front of me but not being able to touch it? Hell on Earth.

"I never lied to you, Taiya," I tilt my head. "I was going to sign them. Until I changed my mind. And I've never lied to you in the past, if you want to get into that right now."

"I'm good, thanks," she says quietly, glancing around the bar. "Nice place."

"Thanks," I say softly. Taiya was with me when we bought the bar, and for the grand opening. It's changed a fair bit since then, as we made more money to do it up. "Did you find an apartment?"

Her eyes flare, surprised. "How did you know I was out looking?"

"Stopped by your house but you were gone. You know I have plenty of room at my place," I offer, adding a charming smile and a raised eyebrow.

Her lip twitches. Such a small gesture, yet the best I've gotten so far. I'm considering it progress. "Sure, live with my ex-husband. I'm sure that's a great idea," she says sarcastically.

"Husband," I correct.

"What?"

"I'm not your ex-husband. I'm your husband," I repeat.

She lifts her shoulder in a shrug, trying to play it off like she doesn't care, but I don't miss the flash of anger in her eyes. "You don't act like my husband, and a piece of paper doesn't change that."

"Ouch," I say, putting my hand over my heart. "I'm glad a piece of paper doesn't change anything for you, because I'm not signing those papers."

She is silent for a moment before she responds. "You never used to be this selfish, Ryan," she says softly, looking down into her drink. My heart hurts in that moment; the pressure actually burns.

"Yeah, well, I used to have you," I reply quietly, now looking down myself. When I glance up at her, she's already watching me. Her eyes speak for her, letting me see much more than she would ever say out loud. I hurt her enough that it perhaps changed her, but *my* Taiya is still standing in front of me.

"You're going to put this on me?" she says, wrinkling her nose. My hand aches to reach out and touch her, to run my finger along the curve of her jaw, my thumb across the bottom of her lip. But I don't. She's not ready for that... yet.

"No. Does it matter?" I ask her, my eyes darting to the door as a customer walks in. She turns her head to follow my line of sight, giving me a glimpse of the tattoo behind her ear. The letter R she got tattooed right after I proposed to her. The letter is in the centre of an infinity sign, and has a little red heart connected to it.

"Sign the papers, Ryan," she says, sounding resigned. I reach out and trace her tattoo with my finger. She shivers at my touch, before pulling away so she's out of my reach.

"We can talk about it over dinner," I suggest, needing to be around her anyway I can. When it comes to her, I will take whatever I can get. She purses her lips but doesn't say yes or no, just flashes me a curious look as she turns to walk out. My eyes follow her until she leaves my sight.

*****

"What are you doing here?" Taiya asks as she open the door to her house.

I try to hide my nervousness and put on a smile. "Last night, you said we could talk. Over dinner."

She gapes. "No, *you* said we could talk over dinner. I didn't respond. My silence was a no."

"Well, you should have been clearer."

"How much clearer could I have been? I don't want to have dinner with you, Ryan. What are we going to do? Reminisce on the old times? Like when you ripped my heart out and stomped on it? That's a good place to start," she says, hurting me with each word.

I swallow before answering, "We had good times too."

She nods once. "Sure we did. But the bad moments kind of overshadow the good ones."

Does she know what she's doing to me with each comment? If she wants payback, she's getting it tenfold. "I don't believe that's true."

"Yes, well, I tried to be a good wife to you. I was always honest, *faithful*, and loyal. I wasn't perfect but I tried my best," she shrugs like it doesn't matter.

"You were perfect," I cut in before she can finish her tirade.

She drops her gaze. "Right, well, I guess perfect wasn't good enough for you."

I sigh, "It wasn't you, Taiya—"

Now, it's her turn to cut me off. "It wasn't me; it was you. Oh, trust me, Ryan. I know it was you. That's why we won't be going to dinner. If you care about me at all, sign those papers. Let me go."

With that parting shot, she closes the door in my face.

CHAPTER
THREE

"I'm this close to forging your signature, Ryan," comes a familiar voice. I stop in my tracks and turn around, grinning when I lay my eyes on her.

"Are you following me now? That's kind of hot," I tease, devouring her with my eyes. It's been a long two weeks since I've laid my eyes on her, and I've been going insane. Trying to stay away, like she wanted, but not being able to get her out of my mind.

"No, unfortunately, the fates are out to get me," she grits out. "Vindictive bitches that they are."

"How so?" I ask, leaning forward. My brow furrows at the expression on her stunning face.

"I didn't know you lived in this building. I just saw Summer and Reid," she says, visibly cringing.

"Are you saying...?" Could my luck really be that good? I try to hide the smile now forming on my lips.

"That I now live on the fourth floor," she says, blinking a few times. She's wearing workout clothes, and has her curly hair tied away from her face. "Reid told me your apartment number," she adds. It's like she read my mind because I was just about to ask that question. She makes it sound like she's going to spend her days avoiding me, but she's here in front of me right now, so I'm not going to complain.

"You living here by yourself?" I ask slowly, hoping the answer is yes. If she's living with a guy, I'm not going to take it so well. I may even go 'Hulk smash' on the bastard.

"Nah, I have a roommate. So listen," she says, changing the subject. "I think we should be civil. Summer invited me out for a drink, and she seems really nice so I'd like to go. Only if it won't make things weird," she rambles, twisting her hands together. I feel like jumping for joy right now. Taiya is going to be around me pretty much every day (considering I'm going to find any excuse to bump into her), and Summer made her feel welcome, bringing her into our inner circle.

Best wing woman ever!

Summer's going to get a lifetime supply of apple juice boxes for this one.

"I think it's great, and I'm glad you're gonna be around," I say truthfully, trying to hide my excitement. I mentally picture myself fist pumping.

Her eyes narrow suspiciously. "We can try to be friends."

"Friends," I reply, trying to keep the venom out of my tone. "Sure," I add, cringing with the lie. Friends is better than her jumping down my throat with her harsh words and throwing the past in my face, like she did the last time I saw her. I would say anything right now to get a second chance with her, and I'm not above playing dirty to get what I want. I'd do anything to go back in time, to be how we were. And I'm not above grovelling.

"Great," she says, a genuine smile appearing on her face. A dimple pops up in her cheek, and my eyes are drawn to it. I fucking love that dimple. I remember when I used to lick the indentation with my tongue.

"So where are you working now?" I ask her, looking away and leaning on the wall of the building. My jeans are suddenly feeling a little tighter than they were a few minutes ago.

Her eyes brighten, and I know she must have found something she loves. Dance. She must have found a job dancing somewhere.

"I'm teaching jazz dance classes at the rec centre," she says, smiling widely. She loves to dance, always has. She's amazing at it too.

"I'll bet you love that," I say fondly, smiling down at her.

She nods her head, and shifts on her feet. "I do. I might not own my own studio yet, but at least I'm still dancing."

Taiya's dream ever since I can remember has been to own her own dance studio.

She glances around. "I gotta head out, but I guess I'll see you around."

"All right," I say softly, watching her walk away.

"Oh and Ryan?" she suddenly calls out.

"Yeah?"

"Sign the papers," she says, waving before she disappears. I grit my teeth at her wanting the divorce so damn badly.

I head to Reid and Summer's, not even bothering to knock.

"Sum!" I call out, walking into the kitchen and grabbing a bottle of water. I shut the fridge with my hip, and turn to see her walk out of her room.

She flashes me a grin and holds her hand to her heart. "I think I'm in love."

"I'd hope so," I say dryly as I open the lid and take a long sip.

"I mean with Taiya! She's so freaking hot," she says, sighing dramatically.

"Don't swoon on me," I tell her with a small chuckle. She's not telling me anything that I don't already know. Taiya is one of those women who will always be beautiful, at any age. She has the sort of beauty to bring a man to his knees. Trust me; I know from experience.

"Hey bro," Reid greets as he walks out of the bedroom. He's bare chested and has a soft look on his face. He definitely just got laid. He leans down and kisses Summer on the forehead, like he hasn't seen her all day, instead of a few seconds. If possible, it makes me miss Taiya even more.

"Did you see her?" he asks.

I nod, and grin. "This building. Really, what are the chances?"

Summer smirks smugly. "Yeah, I might have had something to do with that."

Reid and I both glance at her in surprise. "What do you mean?" I ask warily, leaning back on the counter.

"I may have run into her. I introduced myself, and told her I was Reid's girlfriend, and then mentioned that there was a gorgeous apartment available…" she trails off, wiggling her eyebrows and looking mighty pleased with herself. I shake my head at her, close the space between us and wrap my arm around her shoulder.

"I owe you," I tell her, kissing her on top of her head.

"And I plan to collect," she says with an evil grin. Of course she does.

"What are you two up to? Besides fucking yourselves to death that is. Ouch!" I say as Reid slaps me on the back of my head.

"Summer has classes, but I'm doing nothing. Want to bond?" he asks, uncrossing his arms. He kisses Summer on the mouth, and we say our byes as she walks out. Reid eyes her ass as she departs, clearly enjoying the view. I wonder if they're still in their honeymoon stage or if they are going to be like this forever. For some reason, I'd go with the latter.

"Yeah, I do," I reply, knowing that we're going to end up either playing video games or going to the gym to spar. Truthfully, I wouldn't mind either one right now. Sometimes it just feels nice to have some alone time with my brother to bond.

"Gym?" my brother asks, grabbing a banana out of the fruit bowl and peeling it.

"Sure," I reply. I could definitely use the tension release. I haven't slept with anyone since Taiya slapped me. And I don't think I can consider that as foreplay.

He pauses. "Then I'll kick your ass on the PS4," he pauses, "after I take a shower."

"Plan to lose," I say, smirking.

Reid takes a bite, chews and swallows. "We'll see about that"

"I like a challenge," I tell him, grabbing my own banana and taking a bite.

"Copycat," Reid says, throwing his peel in the bin.

"I'm having a flashback to our childhood," I muse.

The good parts, anyway.

"Right. Shall we go? You can tell me more lame jokes on the way," Reid says, grinning playfully.

My mouth curves into an identical grin.

He loves my jokes.

*****

"Did you bring food?" I ask Summer as soon as she walks into the room.

"Hello to you too," she says, swatting me on the head with one of her books.

My stomach growls. "Reid, make your woman cook," I pout while complaining.

Summer and Reid kiss, and she giggles as he pulls her down onto his lap, abandoning his remote control. Looks like game time is over. I roll my eyes, hoping that they aren't like this around other company. No wonder they don't get many visitors.

"Food's on the table," Summer says when she pulls herself away from Reid, her brown eyes smiling.

Standing up, I grin at her and head straight for the kitchen. When I see exactly what she brought, I walk back into the lounge room scowling. "What is this?" I ask, waving around the bag.

"Salad," she answers, smirking. She pushes away some brown strands of hair off her forehead.

"Since when do we eat salad?" I deadpan. Now don't get me wrong, I will eat salad as a side dish. It's meant to be a side dish, not a whole meal. That's just wrong. I'm not trying out for Australia's Next Top Model any time soon, and my body is in peak shape anyway.

"Clean eating," is all she says. I blink once, before darting my eyes to my brother, who is now outright laughing, his body shaking silently.

"You've lost your balls, brother," I mutter, peering into the bag at the offending salad. All I see is green. A whole lot of green.

"Is there at least chicken in it?" I ask hopefully. I could go for some chicken.

"No," she replies, pursing her lips.

I narrow my eyes at her. "If you wanted me to stop coming here, you just had to say so, you didn't have to go to such drastic measures."

Summer bursts out laughing, almost elbowing Reid in the face as she doubles over. The bastard would have deserved it, but he moves out of the way just in time.

"We're eating healthily, Ryan," Summer says, standing up and walking past me and into the kitchen. I glance back at my brother, who is running his hands through his blond hair. I don't say anything, letting my eyes do the talking for me. Reid's resounding chuckle lets me know he got my message loud and clear. My stomach growls, so I stalk back into the kitchen and make myself a sandwich.

"So when are you seeing Taiya?" I ask her as I slather on some mayonnaise. She opens her salad and forks a piece of lettuce.

"This weekend. I said I'd message her so we can organise something. We'll probably end up going out for drinks."

"She loves to dance," I tell her, a small smile playing on my lips.

"Perfect," Summer beams, lifting the fork to her mouth.

I clear my throat. "Let me know where you guys end up." Summer puts her fork down and pauses, studying me. A slow smile spreading across her mouth.

"You're just gonna show up wherever we are?"

"Yep," I say, popping the P. "Reid and Me will be there."

"Double trouble," she murmurs, taking out a piece of chicken.

I gasp. "There *is* chicken in there!"

She smirks. "Of course there is." Before she can move, I stick my fingers into her salad and pull out a chuck of chicken, shoving it in my mouth.

"Hey!" she snaps, pushing her plate out of my reach.

"Serves you right," I tell her, chewing the piece appreciatively.

"Who knows where your hands have been," she says, raising an eyebrow.

Only on myself. But she really doesn't need to know that.

"I don't think you need to worry about that," I reply in a dry tone.

She grins knowingly. "Never thought I'd see the day."

I run my hands over my jaw, but don't say anything. It's the truth. I want Taiya, and I'm sure as hell not going to ruin any chance I have with her. I still have so much to make up for. I need her to forgive me, for her to let me explain my side of the story so we can move on and finally be together again. There is no other option. Taiya will be mine again.

"What's with the determined look," Summer says, pulling me out of my thoughts.

I tilt my head to the side. "What determined look?"

"This one," she says, trying to mimic my expression. I crack up laughing. She looks more constipated than anything, so I hope I really don't look like that.

"I do not make a face like that," I tell her, speaking the words slowly.

"I don't think you should follow us out. I think you should give her some space. Let her enjoy a girls' night," Summer says, looking thoughtful.

"Not liking that idea."

"I know, but Taiya will have a better night. I don't think she has many friends. She said she lost touch with everyone she used to know."

"She has me. I'm her husband," I add in, watching Summer for her reaction.

She gasps, then smiles, "Yay, you finally told me."

27

Now it's my turn to gasp. "You knew?"

She grins evilly. "I annoyed Reid until he caved and told me."

I shake my head, kind of glad Reid explained so I didn't have to. "I'm sorry I didn't tell you sooner."

"Don't be. I knew you would tell me when you were ready. Didn't think you would blurt it out like that, but you do like to surprise me." She pauses, and stares straight into my eyes. "I'm always here for you, you know that, right?"

"I know that; you're my pole. Here for me whenever I need to lean on someone."

She smiles widely. "How about you use your pole once in a while then?"

"That sounded dirty," I grumble, giving her a small smile.

She laughs. "It did, didn't it."

"Summer!" Reid calls out from the living room.

She instantly stands. "Time for me to make up for skipping the gym today."

"Make up how?"

She wiggles her eyebrows so I understand.

"Oh. Ohhhh. And that's my cue to leave." I kiss her on the head. Just before I let myself out, I stop and turn. "What's Taiya's apartment number?" I call out.

I hope people dropping in unannounced still don't annoy Taiya.

CHAPTER FOUR

Taiya

My roommate Isis walks into my room, a dazed look on her face.

"What?" I ask her, closing my drawer and sitting back down on my bed.

"You have a visitor," she says, grinning. "And a sexy one at that."

I blink twice, slowly. Since moving back to Perth, I hadn't really made any new friends other than Isis and Summer. Isis and I met in one of my dance classes and hit it off straight away. She does the adult jazz/funk class that I teach once a week. When I mentioned that I was looking for a place, she asked me if I was also looking for a roomie. The rest is history. Isis is a bombshell, with a thick head of red hair and pale blue eyes. She has fair skin dusted in light freckles, and a slender yet shapely figure. To sum it up, my roomie is a stunner. I get up and walk around her, walking out of my room to see who could have dropped by. I seriously dislike uninvited guests. I come to a standstill when I see it's Ryan standing in my living room, looking around and taking in every detail of my apartment. I told him we could try to be civil, friends even. However, him dropping by like

29

this wasn't exactly what I had in mind. Maybe a wave to each other in passing? Yep, that was more like what I'd had in mind.

"What are you doing here?" I ask, hating the fact that my heartbeat speeds up at just the sight of him. God, he is still so beautiful, maybe even more so then when I left. Blond, shaggy hair, falling charmingly over his forehead, blue eyes that can see into your soul and a full mouth made for kissing. Ryan Knox is one of the most attractive men I've ever laid my eyes on. I note that he is slightly more muscular than I remember. I can almost make out the outline of his sculptured abs from here.

"Was in the neighbourhood. Just thought I'd drop by and see if you needed anything," he says, smiling faintly.

"How about a divorce?" I say sweetly, so sweet that I'm going to need a filling. I hear a gasp from behind me, and palm my face knowing that Isis heard that little comment.

Ryan smiles. It's the smile that could make women worldwide swoon, and from what I've heard, they have. It seems while I exiled myself in South Africa to lick my wounds, Ryan was busy getting into the panties of any woman he could find. The thought makes me want to curl up in a ball and cry. It hurts. It hurts so fucking bad. Now, instead of letting me move on with my life, he does things like this. Like dropping by, talking with my mum. Hitting Scott, who is nothing more than a friend to me. He's trying to insert himself back into my life, and while I feel the pull towards him more than ever, I can't let myself be vulnerable around him again. Fool me once, shame on you, fool me twice… Ryan and I are over. It seems he is going to still be in my life, but this time around, I'm going to make sure I don't lose myself in him along the way. I used to breathe Ryan. I gave him every inch of me, and in the end, he broke my heart. I won't let him do it a second time, husband or not.

"Nice place," he says, ignoring my comment. I sit down on the royal blue couch, gesturing for him to do the same.

"Is this going to become a regular thing?" I ask with a scowl. I don't want him to feel like he is welcome to drop by anytime he feels like it. I'm trying to rebuild my life back here in Perth and I don't need him messing with my head.

He grins, not phased one bit at the look I'm throwing his way. "Sure it is. A husband likes to spend time with his lovely wife." He pauses, studying me for a moment. "I've noticed you don't even wear your wedding ring anymore."

"We are separated Ryan. Why would I?" I say softly, trying to soften the blow of my harsh words. "Besides neither do you," I add, having noticed it before. I swear the man suffers from a bad case of double standards.

"Right," he says, dragging out the word. He glances down at my hand, as if the ring will magically pop back on my finger. "I guess we'll be seeing a lot of each other."

I purse my lips, unable to hide my agitation. "What happens if you come over and I have someone over?"

The instant the words leave my mouth, Ryan's smile drops and the atmosphere in the room changes, becoming thicker and almost stifling.

"The same thing that happened last time I saw you with a man, I guess," he says flippantly, but I don't miss the underlying threat in his voice. He is unbelievable, he really is. After everything that happened between us, he has no right to act like this. He makes my blood boil.

"I guess I'll just have to find someone who is stronger than you," I reply, trying to keep my face passive.

"Yeah, good luck with that," he replies, the cockiness in his tone igniting me off further. I know for a fact Ryan is a brutal fighter. He hardly ever fights, but when he does...

"Are you here just to piss me off?" I ask, staring straight into his eyes. His hypnotic blue eyes.

"No," he says softly, the heat in his voice dissipating. "I just wanted to see you, is all."

The way he says it, his voice sounding small, makes me feel like the worst person in the world. Yes, I'm trying to save myself, but I don't want Ryan to hurt either.

"Okay. So how's life," I ask him, trying to be friendly. I can do this. I can sit across from this man and act as if he didn't rip my heart out and hand it to me, right?

His lip twitches as I use small talk as my version of an olive branch. "Life is good. How does it feel to be back in Perth?"

"Good actually," I admit. I'd missed my mother, and the reason I actually returned was that she was getting older now, her health wasn't so good. I wanted to be with her, close to her, in case she needed me for anything. Stubborn woman that she is, she won't admit it when she needs help.

"How was South Africa?" he asks, looking genuinely interested. South Africa is like a second home to me. I was born in Capetown, and have visited every year or so since I was a baby. I spent time with my family, especially my cousins, and did a lot of volunteer work to both help out and to keep myself busy. I also worked at my Auntie's clothing store to make some extra money. I spent the year trying my best not to think about Ryan, but no matter the distance, he wasn't far from my thoughts. Which just plain pissed me off. I always said I wasn't going to be one of those girls. Pining away over a man who frankly didn't deserve me. Once trust is broken, there is always a small part of you that won't forget, won't forgive, no matter what you say or how much you try. It really is one of those things that you work hard to get, and can lose in a blink of a second. I wish I was stronger, but I'm not. If I was, I wouldn't be feeling butterflies in my stomach by just being in his presence.

"Good. I enjoyed the change of scenery," I tell him, relaxing back into the plush couch.

"Are you going back any time soon?" he asks, a little hesitantly. My eyes zoom in on his mouth. Oh, that mouth. It always knew exactly what it was doing. Ryan clears his throat, and my eyes move up to meet his. He smirks at me knowingly, clearly feeling more confident after my show of weakness.

I bite the inside of my cheek before I answer, "Nope. I'm here to stay."

"Okay," he says, smiling widely.

I narrow my eyes. "Look, I don't know what your end game is but..."

He raises his hands up in innocence. "Can't I visit an old friend without suspicion?"

"Oh, so now I'm an *old* friend?" I ignore the pang of hurt that his comment incites. This is what I want. I don't have the right to feel upset.

"Well, even before we got married you were my best friend, so yeah. You will always be that to me, even if you're nothing else."

Is he saying that when we get divorced, he still wants to be friends? I don't know how to feel about that.

"Taiya, I'm heading out," Isis says as she walks into the room. She has a backpack hitched on one shoulder, and is dressed in jeans and a loose white top.

"Isis this is Ryan," I introduce.

Isis purses her lips. "Right, the husband. The one you failed to mention."

I sigh. I can feel a long lecture happening in the near future.

"Nice to meet you, Ryan," Isis says, now smiling. She tilts her head to look at me. "I'll be back in a few hours. You want anything?"

I shake my head. "I'm good, thanks. I'll message you if I do."

"All right," she says, blowing me a kiss before walking out. I hear the door lock behind her, making me realise I'm now officially alone with my soon-to-be ex-husband. He must realise it too, because he starts to chuckle softly.

"Want to go out for dinner?" he suddenly asks, after a few seconds of silence. He studies me, anticipating my answer.

"No, thanks, maybe next time," I tell him.

Like when hell freezes over.

"It's just a meal," he says, raising an eyebrow, almost daring me.

"I know that," I say slowly, enunciating each word.

"Then why are you looking like I asked you if you wanted to have sex."

"I'm not," I say quickly, looking down at my black coated nails.

"What are you going to have for dinner then?" he asks, leaning forward with his elbows on his knees. The action tightens his T-shirt along his broad chest, and shows off his biceps. It takes all my will power to look away.

"I'll fix myself something. Don't worry about me, Ryan." Like he hasn't for the past year or so.

"So you learned to cook over in South Africa then?" he asks, smirking at me.

"I might have," I say defensively, sitting up straighter.

"So you can make something other than toast and two minute noodles then?" he asks, doubt evident in his voice.

"Of course I can," I say. I can now fry eggs. So I'm not housewife material, sue me.

"What can you make?" he asks nosily. He's always had an issue with boundaries.

"Lots of things," I lie.

"Such as?" he pries, his eyes dancing with amusement. He's enjoying this, the bastard. He knows I can't cook for shit.

"I really don't think I need to prove myself to you," I huff, crossing my arms over my chest.

He flashed me a megawatt smile. "Do you want me to make you something?"

"Ryan. I'm fine, really."

"Don't be so stubborn, Tay," he says, shaking his head.

Tay.

He used to call me that.

No other woman will ever compare to you, Tay. You're all I see.

I instantly stand up, the pillow that was next to me flying on the floor.

"Okay, you need to go," I say, feeling slightly shaken by the memory.

He stands slowly, but looks confused. "What's wrong?"

"I just… have some things I need to do. I'll see you around, okay?" I tell him, glancing towards my room door longingly.

He rubs the back of his neck with his hand and puffs out a breath. "Yeah okay. Sure." He forces a smile, before turning and walking to and then out the door. I lock it behind him, leaning my back against the door and sliding down it, until I'm sitting on the floor.

Only then do I allow the tears to fall.

CHAPTER FIVE

Ryan

I rest my head against the door listening to her cry. Each sob rips a hole in my heart, each tear lies on my conscience. Instead of walking away and trying to clear my head, I stand there and punish myself by listening to her, because I know I deserve it. She's hurting. I'm hurting. This whole thing is fucked up. We need each other. I just wish she could see it. I could be there for her again, if she'd let me. I want to bang my head against the door, but then she would know I'm still here, standing in front of her door like a fucking creeper. I lift my hand to knock on the door, to beg her to let me comfort her, to hold her in my arms. I pull back my hand before it connects with the door, and instead pull at the ends of my hair, and squeeze my eyes shut. I put my hand in my pocket, fingering my wedding ring. It's on me, where I always keep it. I may not wear it, only because it didn't feel right when I was with other women. I slide the ring back on my finger. When I hear her move away from the door, only then do I do the same.

*****

The next day, I get off my black Harley Fat Boy, and walk into the crowded bar, nodding and smiling along the way at the familiar faces.

"'Bout time you got here," Tag says, throwing a tea towel at my head. I catch it with one hand, grinning at him.

"Isn't Summer meant to be here?" I ask, frowning as I look around.

"She's running late," Tag says, running his hand over his shaved head.

"Did she call in?"

"Reid called in for her," he says, his lips twitching in amusement. "The perks of screwing the boss, eh?" he jokes. A woman walks up to the bar and Tag leans in to hear her order. I chuckle when she flirtatiously pulls at his goatee. He hates that, I know he does, but I don't know why. He gently untangles the woman's fingers and starts to make her drink. I see Rachel walk up to me, a girl I once spent the weekend with. Summer always tells me I have a type, and going by what she says, I guess Rachel would be it. She has a curvy figure, long hair and bedroom eyes.

"Hey Ryan," she coos, smiling up at me.

"Hey Rach, what can I get you?" I ask her, giving her a friendly smile in return.

"One margarita please," she orders, leaning against the bar.

"Sure thing," I tell her, grabbing the glass and commencing to make the cocktail.

"Come home with me tonight?" she asks bluntly, once I've finished making the drink. She bites her lip, giving me a look that says 'I'll make it worth your while.'

I place it down in front of her. "Sorry, can't do, babe." I say it gently, so not to hurt her feelings. I know how much rejection can hurt.

"Why not?" she pouts, pushing away her blonde hair. She doesn't look upset, more like she's confused.

"I'm a one woman man these days," I tell her, grinning. It's the truth. She may not be mine again... yet, but she will be. I don't think a man has ever loved a woman more than I do her, and hopefully, she realises that. If not, hopefully, I can prove it to her.

Her face shows her surprise. "Really? Since when?"

"Since now," I tell her, thanking her as she hands over the money for the drink. I put it in the cash register and pull out her change.

"Hope she knows how lucky she is," she says, accepting the remainder of her money.

"Actually, I'm the lucky one," I tell her, smiling. It's the truth. If only she would let me in, let me see that side of her again. Her vulnerable side. It's not like I expected Taiya to fall back into my arms yesterday, but I guess I was hoping for... something. When I left, hearing her cry ripped my heart out. Those tears let me know a few things. They show just how much I've hurt her, but they also show that she cares enough to maybe work things out. I need to fix the damage I've caused, to show her just how amazing she is. The woman deserves the world, and I plan to give it to her.

Rachel sighs. "I highly doubt that," she says under her breath, before walking back to the table, drink in hand. I smile at her retreating back. If she only knew.

"Can I get a drink or you going to stare at the blonde all night?" comes Xander's amused voice. I turn to my left, smiling at him in welcome. His long hair is tied back away from his face, showing off the ink on his neck. I think he's had even more work done since the last time I've seen him.

"That new?" I ask him, pointing to the side of his neck.

"Yup," he says, sitting down on one of the stools.

"Soon, we aren't going to be able to see any of your skin," I say as I pour him a beer.

"I don't have any on my legs," he says, lifting his shoulder in a shrug.

"Yet," we both say at the same time. I've known Xander for a while now. He's younger than me, but doesn't look it. With his tattoos, muscular build and penetrating eyes, he looks like someone you wouldn't want to mess with.

"How's Jack?" I ask, referring to his dad. I slide him his beer across the table.

"You know Dad," he says, lifting the glass and taking a long sip. "I thought Summer was meant to be here?"

"Yeah, me too. Reid's giving her a late pass," I say, chuckling at my own joke.

Xander tightens his lips. "Sucks not having her at home, so I come to see her and she's not even here."

"She'll be here; don't worry," I say, crossing my arms and watching him. He loves his sister so much it's insane. I guess because she was never always in his life, he doesn't take her for granted now. Xander grew up with his dad, and Summer with her mum. He really is a good man, and I hope he doesn't ever get involved in the things his old man used to.

"Hey," Tag says, walking over to us. I realise he served everyone at the bar while I was here shooting the shit.

"We still on for tomorrow?" Xander asks Tag. Tag grins slowly, and nods. What the hell are these two up to?

"What's happening tomorrow?" I ask, extremely curious. When they both start laughing at my question, I stand up straighter. Now, I really need to know.

"Sorry I'm late!" Summer calls out as she rushes behind the bar. I notice that her hair looks different, lighter or something. We all watch as she rushes to the office and comes back seconds later without her bag. She then walks over to her brother and kisses him on the cheek in greeting.

"What did I miss?" she asks, scanning each of our faces.

"You mean besides work?" Tag says dryly, earning him an elbow to the stomach from Summer.

I chuckle. Summer rolls her eyes, and then leans down to grab an apple juice box from the fridge.

A customer stands at the bar and Tag quickly walks over to serve him.

"So Taiya and I are hanging out next Saturday," she says, poking the straw in and taking a sip. Yes, Reid stocks the bar with her favourite drink.

"Really?" I say, extremely interested. I lean down and wait for her to tell me more.

"I thought we'd start here for pre-drinks then head out clubbing."

"Who's going?" I ask.

"Me, Taiya, her friend Isis and…" She mumbles the last name so I can't understand what she said.

"You, Taiya, Isis and who?" I ask, frowning.

She purses her lips, and then huffs out a frustrated breath. "Reid."

Xander and I laugh. "Reid is tagging along on girls' night?"

"He's… insisting," she says, looking put out. Truth be told, I'm thrilled Reid is going. He can keep an eye on Taiya for me, so I know she will get home in one piece, and no guys will try anything with her if Reid is standing right there. If they value their lives, anyway.

"I thought you wore the pants in the relationship?" I tease, referring to a conversation we had recently. Summer claimed that she ran the show, and from what I've seen, it might be true in certain situations. My brother will do anything to make Summer happy. But when it comes to Summer's safety, Reid does what Reid wants, and I don't think that's ever going to change.

"You gotta choose your battles," she says wisely. Ain't that the truth.

"And you're choosing not to fight Reid on this one?"

"I think it's a great idea," Xander adds in, grinning. He's just as overprotective of Summer, if not worse. "Perhaps I'll tag along too."

"The hell you will," Summer grits out, narrowing her eyes at her baby brother.

"Why not?" Xander says over his pint of beer.

Summer throws her hands up in frustration. "I have no female friends! I'm trying to make one. You guys are all going to scare her off!"

"What about Jade?" I add in, leaning on the table.

"She doesn't count."

"Why not?" I ask, my brows furrowing in confusion.

"'Cos I'm stuck with her. I didn't choose her," she says, making a face.

"I'm pretty sure it doesn't work like that," I say slowly, leaning over and tugging on her ponytail.

She shrugs, pulling her hair out of my reach. "I'm surrounded by you guys twenty-four-seven. It would be nice to have some female company." I grin. I imagine we would get overbearing at times.

"Who are you going out with?" Xander asks, rubbing his fingers over his sun tattoo.

"Taiya and her roommate."

"Is she hot?" Xander asks.

"Who? Taiya?" Summer asks, frowning. She darts her eyes to me as if seeing if I'm gonna jump over the bar and beat the shit out of Xander just for asking.

"No, I've met Taiya. The roomie."

"Isis? Yeah she is beautiful. But she's off limits. Stay away from my friends, Xander, please!"

43

"Why? I'm a decent guy," he says, looking put out. I eye his long hair and tattoos and grin. He will probably scare poor Isis away.

"Yeah, you are. But I'm trying to make friends, and if they hook up with you, it's going to end in disaster."

"What are you trying to say?" Xander asks, narrowing his hazel eyes. These two. It's so amusing to watch them interact.

"I'm saying that you can't have a one-night stand with any of my friends!" Summer says, throwing her hands in the air.

"You hooked up with mine," Xander points out.

Summer purses her lips. "I didn't have a one-night stand with Reid. I'm going to marry the man. It's not the same."

"You just made Isis forbidden fruit," I mutter, shaking my head. Rookie mistake. Does she not know men at all?

Her eyes widen. "I did not," she quickly backtracks, frowning at her brother. "Isis is looking to settle down," she adds quickly, knowing that would probably scare Xander off. Okay, maybe she does know. "Shit, I better go help Tag," she mutters, and I turn to see a group of customers walking up to the bar. As soon as she's gone, Xander raises an eyebrow at me.

"She's pretty," I tell him. And she is. She has nothing on Taiya though, hell, no one does.

"Of course she is," he mutters, but I see him hiding a grin. I refill his glass and then serve a few customers, before heading into the back to try to get some paperwork done. I cringe at the large pile of receipts, turning the laptop on and taking a seat at the desk. Reid walks in an hour later, unable to mask the look on his face. I slowly stand up.

"What's wrong?" I ask, instantly on alert.

Reid sighs heavily, rubbing the back of his head. "Got a letter from Dad."

I clench my jaw, lowering my eyes. "We told him not to contact us anymore."

"He wants us to visit," Reid says, clenching and unclenching his hands.

"Yeah, not going to happen."

"I know. I just thought I'd tell you. You'd get pissed at me if I didn't," he says, watching me closely. I roll my eyes. I'm not going to have a breakdown at any moment, if that's what he's waiting for.

"Heard you're going to the club with my girl?" I say, changing what is a very touchy subject for the both of us.

"Your girl?" he repeats, grinning. The tension in the room evaporates just like that.

"I believe in positive thinking," I tell him, sitting back down in the chair. It creaks as it accepts my weight. Reid looks at me, as if seeing the truth under my cockiness.

"Taiya's a good girl."

"I know she is."

"You need to talk to her about what happened that night," he says, walking over to me and affectionately squeezing my shoulder. A lot happened that night. If I could have a do-over, it would make my life much easier. So many misconceptions and some seriously wrong timing. In the end, I did screw up, especially by not going after her and explaining. Just not as bad as Taiya thinks. She and I were high school sweethearts. We were each other's firsts, and I was hoping lasts. When I proposed at twenty-one, and she accepted, it was the best day of my life. We had a small wedding, with just our close family and friends. Taiya's sister, Claire, was her maid of honour, and Reid was my best man. Everyone said we shouldn't get married, tried to advise us against it, but we didn't listen. We were in love. More than in love. We were head over fucking heels, obsessed, couldn't keep our hands off each other in love. I still feel the same way about her. If anything, absence has made the heart fonder and I crave her more than ever. Back then, we spent as much time as we could together, and we just got each other. I let her in—more than any other person—other than Reid. It's true I kept her protected from a few things in my life, a few things from my past, but that was because I didn't want to taint her with my shit. She was too good for that.

Everything was perfect.

Until I messed up.

After having an argument, I gave Taiya time to calm down, while I gathered my thoughts. I went back the next day, hoping that I could explain everything to her. Except when I went to her mum's house, she informed me that Taiya had left. Left as in, left the country. She had packed a bag, and run to South Africa, where I knew she had family. She did leave me a note. I still have that note, even though I can remember it word for word.

That note broke my damn heart. The words run through my mind of their own accord...

Ryan,

All the best days of my life had you in them. Or maybe they were the best days of my life because you were in them. Either way, everywhere I look, I see you.

You are everywhere.

And everywhere hurts.

That's why I need to leave. Because one look at you and I'll want to forget. Forget what I saw, forget that you took my heart and stomped on it. That you broke me.

I don't know who I am anymore, and that just pisses me off. There is no good way this can end. We both just need to move on with our lives, find out what we want. Well, find out what you want. I knew what I wanted. I just didn't know how to keep it. Move on without me, because I'll be doing the same.

Taiya

"Don't worry, I have a plan," I tell my brother, pushing her words out of my mind. If, not leaving her alone and grovelling, could be considered a plan, well, then, yeah, I had a plan.

"Just be yourself," he jokes, trying to keep a serious face but barely managing. I chuckle at his sage advice, closing my laptop and shoving all the papers in the top drawer.

"Have you spoken to her?" I ask him. Reid and Taiya used to be pretty good friends.

"Well, the first time I saw her she was too busy slapping you across the face," he says, his lip twitching and his eyes alight with amusement.

"Good times," I add dryly.

"The second time I ran into her with Summer, we spoke for a few minutes. It was mainly Summer trying to get Taiya to go out with her. She can be very persuasive when she wants to be," he says, pride evident by the glint in his eyes.

"Yeah, she's a firecracker, that one."

He lifts his shoulder in a shrug. "I thought I'd tag along with them, keep an eye out. Even though I don't fight anymore, you never know what kind of grudges those douchebags could still be holding."

"Shit, I never even thought of that," I mutter, scowling. Reid used to fight in underground MMA, and in the past, things have gotten out of hand with other fighters. Fights have broken out. Once, a fighter made lewd comments about Summer, wanting to start shit; there was no stopping Reid.

"I don't think anything will happen, but you know me, I'd rather be wherever Summer is."

"And you're obviously man enough to admit it," I say, grinning widely.

Reid flexes his ripped biceps. "Anyone have anything to say about it?" he mock threats, showing off.

"I could take you."

He grins, all teeth. "It's adorable that you think so, baby brother."

"Baby? By like, a minute." If that.

"Still counts," he taunts, grinning.

"Are you two done?" came an amused voice at the door. Reid turns around, and I look behind him to see Summer standing in the doorway, her eyes twinkling at our enlightening conversation.

"We will continue this conversation at a later time," I tell Reid, walking past him and nudging him with my shoulder. "Everything all right?" I ask Summer.

"Yeah. Tag just went home so one of you needs to come help out front. But I can see you guys are busy doing something important, so…" she trails off, raising an eyebrow.

"I'm on it. Reid can handle the stocktake," I call out, walking past Summer and exiting the room.

CHAPTER SIX

I don't see Taiya at all over the next few days, and I'm sure that's not by accident. That's why I'm surprised when I run into her on the stairs.

"What are you doing here?" she asks, her brows furrowing. Her curls are piled on her head, and she's dressed in running clothes.

"What am I doing, on the stairs?" I ask, bemused.

"Yeah, you normally take the lift," she says, grimacing when she realises what she just gave up.

"So that's why I haven't seen you around. You've been hiding?" I ask, feeling sad. I had guessed this was what she was doing, but I was hoping I was wrong. I can't believe our relationship has resorted to this. "Taiya, you live here. You shouldn't feel as though you need to avoid me." It hurts; it really does.

She exhales deeply, looking down. "It's just easier, you know."

"I don't want you to feel like you have to do that." I wish I could tell her I'll leave her alone. I wish I could, but I can't. I want to be near her. It's as simple as that.

She glances up at me. "Yeah, you're right. Guess I'll see you around then?"

51

I don't want her to leave. "You want to come over for a bit, so we can talk?"

"Maybe later," she says, her face falling. I see her look down at my hand, and notice that I'm now wearing my wedding band.

She stiffens. "Bye, Ryan."

"Bye," I say softly. I love you. So much it hurts.

With nothing better to do, I head into work, even though today is meant to be my day off.

"What are you doing here?" Jade asks as I walk in, blowing her chewing gum into a bubble.

"Hello to you too," I say dryly, taking in the almost empty bar. We have three customers, which isn't unusual for this hour. "Thought I'd see if you need some help."

Jade looks around the bar. "I think I've got it under control."

"Well, now that I'm here you can do some cleaning," I say, smiling evilly. She pushes her short blonde hair behind her ears, and rolls her eyes.

"I'll get right on that."

When she doesn't move, I pick up the broom and hand it to her. She takes it with a sigh, and walks around the bar. I really need to stop hiring family and friends.

After telling Jade to make sure she does the bathrooms, I wipe the counters clean and stock up the fridge. When the entire bar is sparkling, and I finish all the paperwork, I'm thrilled when Reid texts me asking me if I want to spar with him at the gym. Nothing like keeping busy to distract myself. Tag walks in just as I'm walking out.

"Hey," he says, smiling. I slap him on the shoulder. "Everything all right?"

"Yeah, just came in for a bit."

He looks at me knowingly. "Who's in?"

"Jade."

"Fuck me," he mutters, and I can't help it, I chuckle. Jade can be a huge pain in the ass.

"She probably would," I tell him, just to be annoying. Jade has been eyeing Tag for a while now, but Tag isn't interested in the least. Something about the crazy outweighing the hotness. I think he's been watching too much *How I Met Your Mother*.

"How's Bella?" I ask referring to Tag's daughter.

"She's good," he says, his eyes brightening like they do every time someone brings up his daughter.

"Bring her over, she and River can have a play date again." We did this last month. We took the kids to the beach and had a BBQ with everyone.

"Will do. Better get to work before the boss comes in," he says, smirking.

"Ha ha. See you soon, bro."

I get on my bike, and head straight to the gym.

*****

I walk up the stairs quickly, wanting nothing more than to get home and have a nice hot shower. When I hear the soft laugh of Taiya, I come to a standstill.

"Ryan," she gasps, sounding surprised and a little wary. Standing next to her is the guy I saw her with last time. The one who is still sporting a slight bruise from where I hit him. His face pales when he sees me, glancing to Taiya as if looking for direction. My hands instantly clench, wanting nothing more than to pound him into the ground. It kills me, but I don't. I force a smile, knowing it looks more like a grimace, but it's all I have to offer, and I continue past them up to my apartment. I hear her say my name softly behind me, but I don't reply or look back. I exit the stairway onto my floor, fumbling with my keys as I unlock my front door, slamming and locking it behind me. Pulling my shirt off as I walk into the bathroom, I toss it onto the floor, my shoes and socks following. Taking off my basketball shorts, I turn on the water, letting it run until it's the perfect temperature. Then I stand in the shower, unmoving, replaying seeing Taiya and that fuckhead over and over again.

CHAPTER SEVEN

Taiya

I look over at Scott and sigh. We're sitting on the couch, and I can't take my mind off Ryan. I don't know why I feel guilty, considering Ryan and I are separated and Scott is just a friend, but I do. The look on his face… I scrub my hand down my face, wanting to go and talk to him. I don't want him thinking that I would bring a guy and shove him in his face, even though I don't really have to answer to Ryan. He's been around the block and back while I was away. True, he hasn't shoved any women in my face since I've been back, but does that change anything? I guess it does. To hear about something and to see it is something completely different. Scott is a family friend of mine, and we became close when he came to South Africa on holiday. There is nothing romantic about our relationship, and we've never so much as held hands. I tried to explain that to Ryan the last time, except he was too busy punching Scott in the face. I think Ryan was shocked at seeing me, and took it out on Scott. He held his temper in check today, but I could tell it cost him.

"You going to tell him we're just friends?" Scott says, peeling the label off his beer.

"I'll talk to him," I say. I feel like walking over there right now.

"It's probably a good idea for my health," Scott replies, quirking an eyebrow. My lips twitch. Trust Scott to find something amusing about this situation. "How's your mum holding up?"

"She seems okay, a little tired, but in good spirits," I answer softly. My mum loves Ryan. She was so upset when I decided to leave the country.

Running away won't solve anything, Taiya girl.

Boy was she right. A year later and I still have a husband and a shitload of problems on my hands.

"Fuck. I need to talk to Ryan. Give me twenty minutes, okay?" I tell Scott, standing up and pulling at the hem of my shirt.

"Take your time. I'll catch up on some work," he says, waving his hand. Scott's a really great guy. I lean down and kiss him on the cheek.

"Wish me luck," I mutter under my breath, knowing that I'm going to need it. Closing the door behind me, I take the stairs to Ryan's apartment. I knock twice, shifting on my feet nervously. I knock again before he finally opens it, standing there in nothing but a pair of boxer shorts. I open my mouth, and close it. Only to open it again. "Been working out?" I squeak out, staring at his chiselled six-pack of abs.

"What do you want, Taiya?" he asks, not even amused by my obvious perusal.

"Can we talk?" I ask.

"Oh, now you want to talk. No thanks, I'm really busy right now," he says, moving to close the door. I put my hand on the door, pushing it open and walking past him. I notice his apartment is a hell of a lot nicer than mine, and much more spacious. I walk into his lounge room and flop down onto his couch. "Make yourself at home," he says, an odd tone to his voice. I stare up at him, but his expression shows nothing.

"About before—"

He cuts me off. "You mean you parading your latest fuck around the building?"

I gape. "You hypocritical asshole! You've fucked everything with a pulse, but I can't bring one guy to my apartment?" Okay, totally getting off track here. But the nerve of him!

"I haven't had anyone since you returned, Taiya," he says, sitting down opposite me. "But nice to see you were keeping tabs on me."

"So what? You want a Husband of the Year Award or something?"

His expression darkens, his jaw ticking. "Heaven forbid you say something nice about me."

"Oh, I said something nice about you at the door when I was drooling over your body," I blurt out, not looking directly at him.

"See something you like, did you?" he asks, his tone laced with disdain.

"Are you... offended I was checking you out?" I ask, extremely fucking confused.

His lips tighten, and he pushes his blond hair off his face. "Why are you here?"

"I wanted to tell you about Scott," I start.

"Look, Taiya—"

"He's a friend. Just a friend. He's never even touched me, so stop with the jealous bullshit, Ryan," I get out, cutting off whatever he was going to say. He eyes me suspiciously, as if gauging if what I'm saying is the truth.

"You've never fucked him?"

"No," I snap.

"Kissed him?"

"No, Ryan," I answer patiently.

"He clearly wants you," he says, clenching his fists.

"He doesn't want me, trust me. Just friends. So stop looking at me like I kicked your puppy."

"Of course he wants you, Taiya. What man wouldn't want you?" he says sweetly, and I instantly soften.

"Not everyone feels that way, Ryan," I say softly.

"Then they are blind."

"Are we okay?" I ask, trying to stop my eyes from roaming down to his chest. Smooth, rippled, tanned skin. He's so beautiful it almost hurts. The fact that so many women after me have seen this, have had this man even if only for a night, it hurts like nothing I've ever known.

He clears his throat. "Eyes up here, wife."

"Why? By law doesn't all this belong to me?" I ask, instantly cursing myself for saying that. I seriously can't control myself around this man. It's always been that way.

"Interesting that you say that," he says. As if taking that as permission, his eyes trail over my body for the first time tonight. "As your husband, I want no more males entering your apartment."

"You're kidding me?" I ask.

"Dead serious," he says, his lips curving into a sly smirk.

"Scott's a friend," I say slowly.

"If he has a dick, he's included," he says nonchalantly.

"We're getting divorced. None of this matters."

"That's yet to be seen," he says, studying me under his lashes.

I look around his apartment. "I bet these walls have a few stories to tell."

"Actually, the only woman who's been in here, besides you, is Summer," he throws back, grinning. Clearly happy with himself.

"So you must have moved in recently then," I guess.

Probably just moved in a few days ago.

Silence. Bingo.

"Why did you fuck around so much?" I ask boldly. I need to know the answer to this.

He looks surprised at my question, at the fact that I just spoke about something important. Something addressing the past, something that I didn't dodge. He sighs heavily, leaning back in his chair.

"You left me. I was pissed. I was hurt. My heart was ripped open, Taiya. You obviously didn't give a shit, since you bailed, so I did what I had to do to distract myself." He looks straight into my eyes.

Green clashing with blue. "I'm not proud, or anything like that. It was just my life without you in it."

"Is that what you thought?"

"What?"

"That I didn't give a shit. That's why I left? I left because I loved you so much and you destroyed me. You broke me, Ryan." I needed this reminder. I can't let myself lower my guard around him again. He's my weakness. He hurt me once. Who's to say he won't do it a second time? Am I that desperate for him that I'm willing to give him control over my heart again? I might not be able to heal myself the second time around. I can't run again. I won't let myself.

With that, I stand up and walk out of his apartment, wiping the tears from my cheeks.

CHAPTER EIGHT

Ryan

You broke me, Ryan.

Her words from last night play in my head. This whole situation is so fucked up. How do two people come back from this? Is it true that sometimes love isn't enough? I remember that night like it was yesterday. I was messed up, so fucking messed up. I had just visited my father in prison. I don't know why I went. He'd been calling for years, but Reid and I never went to see him. The last night I had seen him was the night he gave Reid that scar. It was also the night we lost our mother. I went to the prison looking for answers, looking for... something. Redemption from something I'd been carrying around for a long time. Guilt. Something I'd always dealt with, something that made me feel like I wasn't worthy. Like I was a coward.

I left the prison feeling ten times worse than when I walked in. I should have listened to Reid, but I didn't. And then I fucked it up, and lost my wife. I could use many different excuses. I was young. I'd never been with another woman besides Taiya, and the list could go on. But the truth was I fucked up. Plain and simple.

61

"What's with the long face?" Summer asks as she cuts limes into slices.

"Just thinking."

"About Taiya?" she asks, putting the knife down and giving me her full attention. I nod, scrubbing my hands over my face. It's come to the point where we either need to talk, and work on our marriage, or just let it go and move on with our lives. I won't accept the latter, until I've tried my hardest at the former.

"Yeah, we spoke for a little last night," I tell her, washing my hands in the sink and taking over the cutting.

"You ever going to tell me what exactly happened between the two of you?" she asks in a soft voice. I look out over the bar for a distraction, but the place is empty. We don't open for another hour.

"Anything she throws my way I deserve. Let's put it that way." And then some.

"Ryan," she whispers, trying to get me to look at her but I can't. "Everyone makes mistakes." Summer forgave Reid for whatever shit he pulled, but this situation is different. I'm not Reid and Taiya isn't Summer. I don't answer Summer; I'm living in my head and blocking out the world. When Reid arrives with River, I instantly feel better.

"How long do you have him for?" I ask Reid as I lift River in my arms and kiss his chubby little cheek.

"He's staying the night at ours."

"Mia's letting him?" I ask, surprised. Mia normally lets us have River for a few hours max. She's such a bitch. Not that I'd ever say that in front of River.

"Yeah. Mia has a date," he says, telling me with one look all I need to know. Mia wants to get laid, so River is spending the night at Reid's. Not that I'm complaining, I love the little guy.

"Oh, well, our gain," I say, ruffling River's hair. "We better get out of here before the bar opens."

"You want to come to ours?" Reid asks.

"Yeah, I'll wait until Tag gets here then I'll come around." I hand River over to Reid.

"Okay, see you then," my brother says, leaving with Summer and River. Tag arrives half an hour later, and we shoot the shit for a little before I take off.

*****

"Where the hell has Dash been lately?" I ask Reid. We're all sitting in his lounge room, watching cartoons and eating snacks with River. Summer pulled out a whole set of blocks, and other toys to keep him entertained.

"Sorting his sisters out, and working." Shit, I need to drop by his house and see if there's anything I can do to help. Dash has four younger sisters, and does practically everything for them. I can't even imagine what that must be like for him.

"I spoke to him yesterday," Summer adds, earning a scowl from Reid, which she chooses to ignore.

"And?"

"Yeah, he's just been busy. Said he will drop by this week sometime," she says, popping a grape into River's mouth. Summer's going to make an amazing mother someday.

"When's dinner going to be ready? I'm starving."

"Does Taiya cook?" Summer asks, not answering my question. Reid and I burst out laughing.

"Taiya can't even fry an egg."

Summer frowns, like she doesn't like the idea of me not being fed. "Don't worry you can always come here and I'll cook for you."

"I plan on it," I say, pulling her close and kissing her on the cheek sloppily.

"Yuck!" she complains, wiping her cheek with her hand.

"Yuck!" River repeats. We all look at him and grin. He's fucking adorable; he really is.

"No, really. When's dinner going to be ready?" I ask my future sister-in-law. Summer laughs and walks into the kitchen. Reid throws me a 'leave my woman alone' dirty look. I flash him a wide smile. He throws a pillow at me, which I dodge, and it almost hits a lamp.

"What was going on with you today?" he asks, getting straight to the point.

"Nothing," I lie.

"Summer said you zoned out. What's going on in that head of yours?" he asks, looking concerned. Why does he always make me feel so much younger than him?

"Just trying to sort through some things with Taiya," I tell him, being vague.

"I'm always here if you want to talk about it."

"I know, and thank you. I suppose I have Summer to thank for you growing a vagina?" I joke, moving the subject away from me.

Summer chooses that moment to walk in, carrying a tray. "Oh, so a man shows a little emotion and it's a chick thing?"

"No." Yes. "What do you have there?" I ask, peering up at the tray. She puts it in the centre of the table, and I see cheese, crackers, and cold cuts.

"Reid has such good taste in women," I tell her, eyeing the food. Well, except for all the other women he dated before Summer. Summer wrinkles her nose, letting me know she's thinking the same thing. "You're right. He has bad taste; you're the exception."

"I'm sitting right here," Reid growls, pulling Summer onto his lap.

I shield River's eyes. "Keep it PG people!"

The doorbell rings, and Reid gets up to answer the door.

"Are you expecting anyone?" I ask Summer. She shakes her head no. A few seconds later, Xander walks inside, grinning widely. "What's for dinner, sis?"

CHAPTER NINE

"Hello," I say when the redhead answers the door.

"Right, the husband," she smirks. "Hello, come on in." With that, she walks away, leaving the door wide open. I step into their apartment and close it behind me. Walking into their kitchen, I find Isis now sitting on the countertop, eating cereal.

"She's in her room. First door on the right," she says just before she lifts the bowl to her mouth to drink the remaining milk.

I flash her a smile and then turn in the direction she pointed, stopping in front of the first door. I knock, entering when I hear her yell, "Come in!"

"Oh, my God!" she shrieks as I walk in on her standing at the end of her bed in nothing but a towel. My eyes devour the smooth bronzed skin on her bare shoulders. "What are you doing?" she asks, hiking the towel up. It gives me a glimpse of her toned thigh. I try to discreetly adjust my now hard cock, but she notices the movement immediately, and her eyes narrow.

"You told me to come in," is all I can manage to say.

"I said I'm coming, not come in," she growls. Droplets of water run down her arms, and I find myself suddenly feeling extremely thirsty. What wouldn't I give to lick those off her. I notice her eyes widen, as if she suddenly remembered something, and then she slowly steps closer to the bed.

"Okay, you need to leave. Wait in the living room, please," she begs. It's her use of the word 'please' that has me instantly suspicious. My eyes give her a once over before moving to the bed. It's then that I see what she didn't want me to. I glance over at her, amused, chuckling when she turns red.

"I could take care of that for you, you know," I tell her, gesturing towards the hot pink vibrator.

"Someone kill me," I hear her mutter under her breath.

"Well, you know, an orgasm is known as the little death, so…" I trail off, letting my remark hang in the air.

"Ryan."

"Yes," I say, unable to rein in the huskiness of my voice. She is so fucking beautiful. Even more so than I remember, if that's even possible. How is that possible? My tongue peeks out over my bottom lip, and her eyes are glued to my mouth. I know she wants me, that has never been an issue, but I want her head and heart in the right place. I don't want her to regret anything we ever do together.

"Ryan," she repeats, swallowing hard. I walk over to her, closing the space between us in a few steps.

"Your hair is dripping," I say softly, grabbing the slightly damp towel off the bed and using it to dry her hair a little more. "You'll get sick." As gently as I can, I rub the towel over her hair, concentrating on the dripping ends. She waits quietly, but I don't miss the stiffness of her posture.

"Can we talk?" I ask her, removing the towel and placing it back on the bed.

"What about?" she says, tilting her head back to look at me. Her wide green eyes peer up at me. Fuck. Those eyes. They entrance me.

"About us," I say, my gaze not leaving hers. I need her to know I'm serious about this. About fixing us, this mess I created. I want my wife back. Suddenly, she spins around and takes a single step closer. She smells fresh, like soap and strawberries, and her hair is already starting to spring back into curls as it dries.

"Look, I don't think…"

I reach out and frame her face with my hand, cutting off her objections. "Then don't." I lean forward and kiss her softly on the lips, unable to stop myself. I know I shouldn't, but fuck, I want her so damn much. My heart is thumping out of my chest. I've wanted this moment for so fucking long; it almost hurts to finally have it. I don't ravish her mouth like I want to. Instead, I hold myself back and kiss her gently, so scared that she will push me away. She responds timidly, opening her mouth for me so I can enter. I groan as our tongues touch, revelling in the scent of her, the taste of her. She lifts her arm up to hold onto my bicep, allowing the towel to fall onto the floor. My gaze instantly drops, and I get harder than I think I've ever been in my life. Reaching my hand behind, I grip her hip and pull her closer, rubbing my rough fingers over her smooth, creamy skin. A sigh escapes her mouth as I trail kisses down her jawline, sucking gently on her earlobe.

"Tell me you want this," I whisper into her ear. I told myself I wasn't going to, but now I can't make myself stop.

"If I do, are you going to hold it against me?" she whispers back. I lift my head up so I can look into her eyes.

"What do you mean?"

"If we do this, it doesn't mean anything. We're not in a relationship. We aren't working on our marriage. We are just... it's a one-time thing," she manages to get out, lifting her chin up stubbornly. Her mouth is saying one thing, but her eyes another. That's probably the only thing that's stopping me from walking out of this room right now. She presses her breasts against me and my cock twitches.

Well, not the only thing.

I step forward, taking her with me until the back of her knees hit the bed. I lift her up by her ass, enjoying the sound of surprise that escapes her pouty lips. She grips my shoulders with her hands, holding on for dear life. I gently lay her back onto the bed, keeping my eyes locked with hers the entire time. Even guarded, her eyes are beautiful green pools I could get lost in. Great, she's turning me into a fucking poet. Pulling back from her body, I let myself take her in completely. Breasts that overflow my hands, a tiny waist and flared hips that are perfect to grip onto. Utter perfection. She watches me studying her, but doesn't say anything, just allows my silent perusal. Leaning forward, I cup her face and capture her lips, more demanding this time. My fingers roam towards her breasts, feeling the weight of one in my hand before swiping the nipple with my thumb. She moans loudly, rubbing herself against me, encouraging me to give her more. I smile against her lips, giving her one more kiss before moving my head down. I take my time, kissing her jaw, her neck, and her shoulders. I run my tongue down in between her breasts, holding them both in my hand. I suck one nipple into my mouth, using my tongue and then my teeth to tug gently. Taiya's hands run through my hair, pulling the ends, telling me she wants more. I glance up at her as I lick her other nipple, knowing that it needs my attention too. When I have her writhing on the bed in pleasure, I head further south, nibbling around her belly button before reaching her bare pussy. I run my hands over her thighs, squeezing gently before spreading them. My cock strains against my jeans as I see her core, wet and ready for me. I kiss up her thighs, and the closer I get, the more I take in her scent. It's just as I remember. As soon as her taste hits my tongue, I groan. Using her ass cheeks to pin her down to the bed and keep her in place, I devour her. This is what an alcoholic must feel like when they have a drink after being sober for so long. She does that to me. It isn't long before her thighs start to tremble and she's calling out my name. Could it get any better than that? She knows who is between her legs, giving her pleasure. She knows who in this minute, she belongs to.

"Fuck," she curses as I suck on her clit, prolonging her release. Her hips buck wildly, and I watch her every movement, enthralled. When she finally collapses onto the bed, her tension released, I give her one last lick before I pull away. I stare at her as I wipe my mouth with my hand, her beautiful body not doing much to help my straining erection. When I push off the bed and stand up, she looks up at me in confusion.

"What are you doing?" she asks, her voice hoarse.

"I'm not going to make love to you until you admit that you're mine, and I know you aren't ready to do that right now," I tell her honestly. My dick protests, but for once, I ignore him and walk towards her door. I open it, turning back to face her. "I love you, Taiya," I tell her. Then I walk out.

CHAPTER TEN

"Has Reid seen what you're wearing?" I ask Summer, raising a sceptical eyebrow.

"What's wrong with what I'm wearing?" she says, looking down at her tight white dress.

I make a choking sound. "I can see... *everything*."

She rolls her eyes. "Since when do you care about seeing too much of a woman?"

"It's you. It's a little different. You're not just any woman. You're my future sister-in-law," I complain.

Summer laughs at my sullen expression.

"And Taiya is going out with you. You both don't need the added attention," I tell her, scowling. Maybe I should go with them?

"You're not coming with us. Taiya will be pissed," she says, reading my mind. "Besides, Reid will be there, so stop worrying. And yes, Reid saw this dress. Why do you think it took me so long to get ready?"

I choose to ignore her comment, leaning back into the couch. Summer leaves the room, I assume to primp herself and I glance at the door once more, wondering when she's going to arrive. I haven't seen Taiya since the other day, when I walked out of her room and left her alone and naked. I went home and

73

had three cold showers that night. Yes, three. I know Taiya; she would have let me make love to her, and then she would have pushed me away. I don't think I could have taken it if she said it was a mistake. When I do make love to her, she will be ready to accept that we were made for each other. My brother walks into the room, wearing jeans and a black shirt. My eyes narrow when I realise it's *my* black shirt. His hair is still damp from his shower. He looks at my expression and grins.

"A little jealous, are we?" he teases, running his hands through his hair.

"I could come, you know."

"And ruin Taiyas's girls' night?"

I exhale loudly. "Never mind, I have a million things to do tonight anyway," I lie. I have nothing to do. At all. I already cleaned the apartment this morning, so I can't even do that. I suppose I could watch some TV, or something. Animal Planet might have a documentary on. For once, that doesn't even sound appealing.

"Like what? Sit at home, watching Animal Planet and wishing you were out with Taiya instead?" he says with a smirk.

Sometimes it sucks that my brother knows me so well. Reid looks at me, and I don't know what he sees, but his expression softens.

"It's just a night out. I won't let her out of my sight," he says. He's thinking I'm worried about her with other men. And while the thought kills me, it has been a year and she obviously would have been with someone else in that time. The thing that I'm so out of sorts about is that she will be there with my favourite people. Reid and Summer. Shouldn't I be there too? My brother, my best friend and my wife are going out and I'm stuck at home. I feel like I'm a kid being put in the naughty corner.

"I know," I say, forcing a smile. Reid shakes his head at me, leaving the room. The doorbell rings a few seconds later, and I instantly stand.

"I'll get it, Ryan. Don't you move," Summer says as she enters the room, walking like a professional in her high heels. I hear the door open, and the sound of Taiya's voice. A few seconds wait, and then the object of my obsession steps into the living room. Caramel curls frame her face, bouncing with each step. She's wearing makeup on her face, but not too much, thank fuck. A short black dress that shows off her thighs, and sparkly silver high heels. Images flash in my head about the things I want to do to her wearing nothing but those heels. Her emerald eyes widen when they see me, and then narrow.

"Ryan," she says curtly, nodding her head.

"Hey Tay," I say, taking in the beauty that is my wife. She gives me a weird look, one I can't decipher. I used to be able to tell exactly what she was thinking. I wish I could just walk up to her and touch her. Hold her. Kiss those perfect lips. Isis steps in behind her, giving me a smirk and a small wave.

"Hey Isis."

"Have a seat, girls. I'll just be a sec," Summer says, walking back into the bathroom.

"Do you girls want a drink?" I ask politely.

"Yes, please," Taiya says, sitting down on the couch. "Whatever you have is fine." Before I can go into the kitchen to get them something, Reid walks in holding a bottle of vodka, ice and orange juice.

"Hey Reid," Taiya greets. "This is my friend Isis. Isis this is Reid." Isis says hello, and I can see her plainly checking my brother out. Yeah, good luck with that one. Summer returns with a tiny little bag in her hand, takes a seat and starts talking with Taiya and Isis. I can tell she's a little nervous. She's not exactly a people's person. I grin when she finishes her drink in a few gulps. Isis, on the other hand, chats away animatedly, like she's known Summer her whole life. Taiya is a little more reserved, but still friendly. I see her looking over at me out of the corner of her eye. I don't remove my gaze from her. When she walks into the kitchen to put her glass away, I take my chance.

"You look beautiful," I tell her, leaning against the kitchen table. I can smell her from here, so fucking sweet.

"Thanks," she says, not looking at me.

"You mad about the other day?" I ask, frowning. Didn't she understand why I didn't finish what we started?

"Yeah, I just love getting left naked and willing," she mutters, finally turning around to look at me.

"Hey, I got you off," I say, wincing when I realise how asshole-ish that sounds.

Her eyes narrow to slits, which seems to be her most common look when she's around me. "You know what, you made the right decision. No good is going to come from us fucking each other."

Ouch. "I didn't want you to regret it after, Tay. It would kill me," I say softly, letting my guard down for a minute. For her to see how much it actually killed me to walk away. "We need to talk before anything like that happens."

"So what, you have rules now? Going down on me is okay then?" she says, putting her hands on her hips. Her lips are a plump pink, and I can't keep my eyes off of them.

"Are you complaining about me going down on you?" I ask, rubbing my jaw with my fingers. Will I ever figure women out? I'm assuming the answer to that is a resounding no.

She huffs and tries to walk around me, but I gently take her by the wrist. "Tay," I whisper. She stills and looks at me. I mean *finally* looks at me, and sees me.

"Ryan," she whimpers, letting her guard down. I pull her into me, wrapping my arms around her.

"You go out and have a good time tonight, okay? Will you talk to me tomorrow? I mean actually talk to me, Tay?" I'm practically begging, but I don't care. There's nothing I wouldn't do to get her back.

"Okay," she says, and that one word gives me hope. So much fucking hope, I feel like jumping for joy.

"Okay," I repeat, kissing her gently on her lips. Just as she pulls away, Summer walks in, smiling widely as she takes us in. I can almost feel the happiness pouring off her in waves.

"Ready to go?" she asks Taiya, who nods. Taiya turns around and offers me a sweet smile before walking out of the kitchen. Summer gives me a thumbs up.

Such a dork.

*****

A timid knock at the door makes me cease my workout. I do another five push-ups and then walk briskly to the door, opening it widely without even bothering to look through the peephole.

"Long night?" I ask a tired looking Taiya. Her hair is piled on her head, unlike before she left, and her eye makeup a little smeared. She still looks fucking beautiful. I see her eyes roam over my bare chest hungrily, and I wait quietly as she takes her fill.

"You could say that. We got in a few hours ago and I fell asleep on Summer's couch," she says as she finally looks up, wrinkling her nose.

"Why didn't you go home?" I ask, considering she lives in the same building.

"Summer insisted I come over and give her a few dance lessons," she says, shaking her head. "It's a long story."

I'll bet it is. I realise we are standing there talking at the door, so I quickly invite her in. She walks in barefoot, carrying those sexy shoes in her hands.

"Want some water or juice?" I ask her as she walks into the kitchen.

"Not juice," she says, her face paling.

I grin. "Too many screwdrivers last night, huh?"

"I never want to drink orange juice again," she says, her tone deadly serious.

I laugh. "You never want to drink orange juice again? How about never drinking vodka again?"

She looks at me like I'm crazy. "Let's not say anything we can't take back, Ryan," she says, putting her hands up in a 'calm down' motion. I get her a bottle of cold water out of the fridge, open it and hand it to her.

"Still fucking crazy I see," I murmur as she gulps the water down. I stare at her delicate neck and throat as she swallows. To me, Taiya is as she's always been. A perfect mixture of sweet and feisty, and so full of life.

She puts the bottle down and raises an eyebrow. "You getting old, Ry?"

"Is that a challenge?" I ask her. "Honestly, I don't drink much. Working in a bar has put me off."

"Me either," she admits. "Dancing and drinking don't mix."

"Really?" I scoff.

She laughs, and the sound is music to my ears. "I mean teaching dance classes, being a dancer and wanting to be my best physically, and drinking don't mix," she clarifies.

I give her an obvious once over. "You sure are at your peak."

She makes a tsk tsk noise, before her expression clears. "I believe you wanted to talk."

"I did. I mean, I do," I say, the air in the room changing. Gone is the light conversation, and something deeper and darker takes over. I clear my throat. "I think we need to start at the beginning."

She tilts her head. "What is there to say? We were high school sweethearts, got married earlier than we should have. You never got to sow your wild oats, so you did it behind my back when we were married," she says, shrugging like it's no big deal, but I don't miss the flash of pain before she's able to mask it.

"I never cheated on you, Taiya," I tell her, being completely honest.

"Right," she scoffs. "You wanted to have your cake and eat it too. What, a nice little wifey at home, and some bitch on the side?" she yells, her cheeks flushing in anger. She stands up. "Do you know what? Fuck, this was a mistake."

"This is déjà vu, isn't it? You turning your back on me, walking away without giving me even one minute to explain," I snap, losing my composure, desperate for her to hear me out.

"Well, as soon as I left, you just proved my theory, didn't you? Having sex with anyone, proving to me that that's what you really wanted! The few friends I had in school loved to tell me on social networks exactly what you were getting up to. After a while, I shut everything down and cut them all out of my life because I didn't want to hear anymore!"

"Is that what you think?" I ask her, my eyes widening in shock.

She puts her hands on her hips. "What else am I supposed to think? Your actions speak louder than words, Ryan." This is the conversation we should have had a long time ago. These are old wounds resurfacing and still causing lasting damage. Still inflicting pain.

"I made a mistake by pushing you away, but I never slept with anyone until you left me," I say softly, but with conviction. I rub the bridge of my nose when I look at her face, knowing that she still doesn't believe me. "Have I ever lied to you before?"

"Not that I know of," she says, biting her plump bottom lip.

"It's because I didn't lie, Tay. I still messed up," I admit, swallowing hard. "She kissed me; that's it. I swear."

"I know she did, Ryan, because I saw it," she says, her beautiful green eyes pooling with tears.

"What?" I ask, dreading the answer.

She stands. "I have to go," she whispers, not looking directly at me.

"Tay, don't go, please," I beg, coming closer to her.

She puts her hands up to stop me. "I feel like I'm right back there, watching the love of my life kissing *her*. Why did it have to be her?" she says, in a low tone that scares me. She glances up at me, her eyes lacking their usual sparkle. "Now I remember why I left. You're a fucking asshole, and you broke my heart."

"It was just a kiss," I tell her, reaching out and pulling her into me. She stills, but doesn't push me away. Thank fuck she doesn't, because I don't think I could handle that right now. "Just one kiss, a mistake. Biggest mistake in my life because I lost you."

"Biggest mistake because you got caught, more likely," she says into my chest. Does she really think of me like this? Does one stupid kiss, because I was messed up that day, turn me into an untrustworthy cheater in her eyes? Will I be branded that way forever? I'm going to show her, prove to her that she's the only woman I will ever want.

"Forgive me," I whisper into her ear, running my hands down her arms.

"I really think we should finalise the divorce and move on with our lives, Ryan," she says, unable to look me in the eye as she speaks.

"And I think we should fight for each other, because we both deserve that. We owe it to each other Tay, to try and fix this," I say, silently pleading that she wants to try and work on us. I can fight for the both of us, but I want her to want this too.

"I don't know, Ryan," she says, sighing dejectedly. She smells like apples, with a hint of alcohol and smoke. "Have you been smoking?" I ask, surprised. Taiya used to hate smoking with a passion.

"I may have picked up a habit or two," she admits, nuzzling my chest. "Can we talk about the rest of this later? I just want to go home, have a shower and sleep."

"Okay, come on. I'll walk you home."

CHAPTER ELEVEN

Taiya

I rub my forehead, willing the headache away. Why did I drink so much last night? Oh, right, I was both trying to not think about Ryan and gathering courage to finally face him at the same time. I roll over, digging my face into my soft feather pillow. Luckily, I don't have to work today, and I don't have anything planned apart from cleaning my apartment and dinner with my mum.

The talk today with Ryan didn't go as I'd envisioned. I wanted to keep him at arm's length, listen to his excuses, but not let them change my mind about not wanting to be with him. The bottom line was that I saw him, with her wrapped around him, their lips connected. I can't get that picture out of my head, no matter how much I want to. Some other women might feel differently, and think, well, it's only a kiss. But to me, it was something more.

Ryan and I were each other's first kisses. Until that moment, I was the only woman he'd ever kissed. Maybe that was why he did it. Maybe he wanted to experiment, to see what it was like to kiss another woman. I don't know what was going on in his head, and the truth was, I never let him tell me so I could

83

figure it out. I know I should have heard him out, been rational, but after witnessing that, I kind of blocked it out. My walls instantly went up, and to be honest, I kind of felt sorry for myself. Was it something I did? Why her? All these kinds of questions ran through my head, and then after a while, I just got plain pissed off. No, it wasn't my fault. No there is nothing wrong with me. It was his decisions, and his actions, his mistake. I don't control his actions, he does. I like to think of myself as a strong woman, so when I started questioning myself, I felt as though I was losing myself. Like I had become weak, and so dependent on Ryan that I couldn't function without him. That's why I left. I needed to get away, sort my shit out, and stop sulking. Women's hearts get broken every day. So I became a statistic. Other women got through it, and so could I. Our conversation resurfaced old wounds, and we didn't even get to finish it.

Stretching my arms over my head and arching my back, I slide into a sitting position. Last night was really fun. It was so good to catch up with Reid, and Summer was a blast. Reid really hit the jackpot with that one. Isis had a good time too, if the table dancing was any indication. I'm surprised she ended up going home alone after all the male attention she was getting. One guy tried to get grabby with me and Reid quickly stepped in, handling the situation like a pro. I don't think anyone with a penis dared to even look at Summer with the protective vibes Reid was throwing off. I've never seen him act like that before in all the years that I've known him. I think it's freaking cute how he calls Summer 'beauty,' and he's also majorly bulked up and now looks like a badass. I made him dance with me to one song, and when it was over, he spoke to me about Ryan. There, in the middle of a club, we have a deep and meaningful. I love my brother-in-law. Reid and I had always been close, throughout high school, and after, when Ryan and I married. It sucked having to cut him out of my life when I left Ryan. I thought he'd be mad at me, but surprisingly he wasn't.

I force myself to get out of bed, and head straight for the kitchen.

"Good morning," Isis says, her voice thick with sleep. She's wearing a plain white T-shirt that reaches mid-thigh and that's it.

"Morning," I mumble, grabbing some water out of the fridge.

"Did you have fun last night?" she asks, eyeing me curiously.

"I did. You?" I ask, after I swallow a mouthful of water.

She chews her toast and swallows before she replies, "I had a blast."

"Yes, the table dancing kind of gave that away," I tease, my lips curving slightly.

She laughs. "Good times."

"I'll bet. I saw you talking to Tag," I say, lifting my brow.

"How fucking hot is he?" she says, her eyes flaring. "How did it go with Ryan? I hope you guys made up."

I guess my silence was answer enough. "Seriously?" she says slowly, dragging out the word.

"It's complicated."

"I bet Tag's really uncomplicated," she says, a dreamy look on her face.

I laugh, knowing how far from the truth that is. "Did he seem interested?"

"Do you even have to ask me that?" she says, mock pouting.

"Sorry, I forgot how modest you were," I tell her, my voice laced with sarcasm.

She blinks at me twice. "Is that an old shirt of Ryan's?" she asks, staring at my T-shirt. It used to be his favourite T-shirt and I took to sleeping in it. I still do.

My face heats. "Yes."

"You have it bad, girl," she says, shaking her head.

I clear my throat. "We'll see."

"What's the plans for today?" she asks, cutting up a mango.

"Cleaning, remember. Then I'm going to check on Mum and have dinner with her."

She sighs heavily, "I hate cleaning."

"I know you do." That's why I never go into her room unless it's a life or death situation. On the plus side, she's pretty handy in the kitchen, so I don't mind picking up her slack with cleaning, because she picks up mine with cooking.

I glance at the time. "It's already one, holy shit."

"I know. We need longer to recover. Not as young as we used to be," she says, biting the little squares she made on her piece of mango.

"That mango looks good."

"Want some?" she asks, grinning.

"Yep," I say, popping the P, my eyes not leaving the fruit. A knock at the door startles me, diverting my attention. Isis and I stare at each other before looking down at our T-shirts and panties. Clearly we aren't dressed for company. I shrug, and walk to the door, opening it about an inch.

"Hey," I say, taken aback. I didn't expect to see him again so soon.

"Hey, can we talk for a second?" he says, looking a little unsure.

"Ummm," I mumble, before making a second decision and opening the door.

"Nice T-shirt," he says, grinning as he walks into the house. Well, shit. If that didn't give me away, I don't know what will. I clear my throat, and avoid looking into his knowing eyes.

"Hey Isis!" he calls out to my roommate. She calls out a hello in return.

"No need to yell," I tell him, wincing as my head pounds.

"Sorry," he apologises, staring at my thighs. He doesn't sound sorry at all. We walk into my room and sit down on the bed. I can't help but remember the last time we were alone in this room together, and I can feel the heat rise up my neck. That was pretty fucking embarrassing.

"Is everything okay?" I ask, confused as to why he's here. I'm pretty sure we said what we needed to, and although there was a lot more we needed to discuss, I still needed time to think things over.

"Yes, I just forgot to do something when I walked you to your door."

"What?"

"This," he says, cupping my face in his hands and capturing my lips in a kiss. Not just any kiss. He's telling me something with this kiss; I can feel it. I understand it. The emotion, the... love. It's undeniable. My tongue slips out to taste his, timidly at first. When I turn to straddle him, he pulls away, eyes shining.

"That was some kiss," I gasp, breathless.

He smiles widely, showing off his perfect straight teeth. "I'm glad you approve."

"He just kissed me into submission." When he starts laughing, hard, I realise I've said that out loud.

I don't have time to feel embarrassed because he stands up, leaning over me to kiss me on my forehead. "I'm going into work. You know where to find me whenever you want to finish that conversation."

With that, he exits the room, leaving me more confused than ever.

CHAPTER TWELVE

Ryan

It's been two weeks and Taiya still hasn't come to me. I thought I was making the right decision, putting the ball in her court, not so patiently waiting for her to come to me. We've seen each other in passing, and even spoken a few times, discussing everything except what we should be. *Us.* I want her back with me, moving in with me in my apartment. At least she hasn't mentioned the divorce papers, so I guess that's something at least. I look at the time, wanting to go home. It's been busy all evening, and I have an hour until Reid gets here so I can go home early. When Summer walks into the bar with Taiya, I know that my luck has changed. She hasn't stepped in my bar since the night she and Summer went out. She is a sight for sore fucking eyes. She's wearing jeans, so tight they are like a second skin, and a peach-coloured top, showing off a hint of cleavage. I couldn't stop the smile on my face if I wanted to.

"You're here," I blurt out. Does this mean something?

"Yeah, Summer insisted we come out for a drink," she says, and my hope plummets.

I look down to mask my disappointment. "Right, of course. Summer, your usual?"

"Yes, please, Ry," she says.

"Taiya, how about you?"

"I'll have the same please," she says, sitting down in front of me on the stool. I make them two vodka sunrises and place them in front of them. Not accepting Taiya's money, I'm almost insulted she would think I would ever expect her to pay. Hell, this business is hers too if she wants it. Reid walks in earlier than I expected him to, obviously because Summer's here. He kisses Summer, says hi to Taiya, and then walks around the bar.

"What, no hello for me?" I say, clasping my hand over my heart.

Reid pinches my cheek. "Feeling left out, are you?"

"Yes," I say, playfully pouting. Reid puckers his lips and brings them towards my cheek in slow motion. I step out of the way in time and elbow him in the stomach.

"You perve, at least take me out on a date first," I joke. I see Reid's smile turn into a frown, and follow his line of sight. Seeing Mia walk into the bar, I wonder what the hell she's doing here.

"You want me to deal with her?" I ask, seeing Reid staring at Summer. I don't wait for him to reply. Instead, I walk out and meet Mia halfway.

"Is River okay?" I ask instantly.

"He's fine. I'm just here for a drink," she says, pursing her bright red lips.

I cross my arms over my chest. "Really? Out of every bar in the city, you decide to come in here?"

She rolls her eyes. "I'm not here to cause any trouble, Ryan." She reaches out and puts her hand on my bicep. "I'm seriously just here for a drink." Before I can answer or remove her hand, Taiya walks up and stands next to me. She puts her arm around my waist possessively, and stares at Mia.

"Everything okay here?" she asks, lifting one of her dark eyebrows.

"Fine," I say, leaning down to kiss the top of her head. I take advantage of the moment and put my arm around her, pulling her into my body.

"Hello Taiya," Mia says, lips curling is distaste. I almost forgot these two knew each other.

"Mia. I understand you've been with the other two Knox men, but you won't be getting your claws into this one," Taiya says softly, but her voice is laced with steel.

I grin at her comment, and look up at Mia. "Give me a second."

She walks past us and sits at the bar, right next to Summer. Great.

"You never came to see me," I tell her, getting straight to the point. She tries to look down so I gently lift her chin up with my thumb. "Why?" She mumbles something I don't hear. "What did you say?"

"I said, I'm scared," she says, so softly that I have to strain to hear her.

"You don't need to be scared, beautiful," I tell her. It kills me that she feels like this, but I know if she gives me the chance, I can fix our marriage. "I want nothing as much as I want you, Tay. I'm not going to mess anything up this time. You need to give me a chance to prove myself," I tell her. She licks her bottom lip, before giving me a slight nod. I exhale heavily, feeling relief and hope pour through my system.

"You won't regret it," I tell her, before kissing her gently. I take her hand into mine, intertwining our fingers and walk her back to her seat. Reid has served Mia her drink, and is leaning over the bar talking with Summer, their foreheads almost touching.

"You want me to take you home?" I ask her.

"Are you going now?" she asks, and I nod. "I'll come with you." It feels like Christmas morning. We say our byes and I walk her to my bike. I pick her up by her curvy hips and place her on, putting the helmet over her head. The curls sticking out from underneath make me smile. Nothing can fully contain that hair of hers. I slide my leg over and hop on. Taiya holds on tight, her arms around my stomach, gripping onto my abs. I have one last thought before I ride off.

This is exactly where I'm meant to be.

*****

"I thought you were taking me home," she says as we walk into my apartment.

"I am," I reply, closing the door behind us. She spins around to face me, studying me for a moment.

"You really want to make our marriage work?"

"More than anything," I tell her, taking her by the hand and leading her to my bedroom. I turn the knob, opening the door, then pick her up and carry her to my bed. Laying her down gently, I lean down and take off her shoes for her, putting them neatly in the corner of the room. I take off my own, and then jump into bed with her. We lay side by side, both staring at the ceiling. I reach out and grab her hand with mine, absently drawing circles with my thumb on her palm.

"Do you believe me?" I ask. She knows exactly what I'm referring too.

"Yes, I do."

"But?" I ask, sensing her hesitation.

"It's not as simple as that, is it?" No, I guess it isn't.

"Are you ready to listen?" I ask her. She nods, turning on her side to face me. So I tell her. I tell her how I went to see my father, all the things he said to me. How he told me I was a coward. How I will never be the man Reid is. I tell her how the night Reid got his scar, he was defending our mother from our father, and how I was too scared to do anything about it. Reid's scar is proof of his courage, and of my cowardice. It's my shame to bear, and I'll live with that for the rest of my life.

Who the fuck would marry you, son? She's going to figure out you're worthless sooner or later.

"Ryan, you were a kid," she says, squeezing my hand. I shrug, because really that isn't an excuse. Not in my eyes.

"When I got back home, Sarah was waiting at the door. She said she was there looking for you. I let her in, and then she started hitting on me. I was numb. I wasn't thinking. She kissed me, and yes, I kissed her back. It was different. Not even good different, just

93

different." I clear my throat, not wanting to continue, but knowing I have to. "She took her top off, and I knew that it wasn't what I wanted, or who I wanted. I told her to get dressed and get out. Instead, she threw herself on me and that's when you walked in. The look on your face. I couldn't believe what I was doing, Tay. You were and are everything to me. I don't know what was wrong with me. I was such a fuck up, just like he said." I look over at her to see her staring into space, her face expressionless. "I'm so fucking sorry, Tay."

"So, would you have continued if I didn't walk in?" she asks, her voice small. I bring her fingers to my lips and kiss them.

"No, Tay. No," I tell her, my eyes pleading with hers to believe me. "And then you left me. You just left, without letting me explain."

"I need some time to think," she says, sliding off the bed and standing up. She grabs her shoes and then walks out without looking back.

But what did I expect?

I just told her in detail what happened between her ex-best friend and me.

CHAPTER THIRTEEN

Taiya

"Really great work, Lisa," I tell her after she finishes the dance routine.

"Thanks, Miss Rose!" she answers, smiling proudly. She's ten-years-old and a born dancer. It makes me feel alive just watching her, and knowing she loves to dance as much as I did when I was her age, as much as I still do. I wait until the last child is picked up, and then lock up the studio. I slide into my car and drive home. I haven't spoken to Ryan since last week, when he opened up to me and told me everything that went on back then. I still can't believe of all the women, it was Sarah, my childhood best friend that tried to make a play for my husband. I haven't seen Sarah since I returned, and I hope I never do.

I never spoke to her after the incident, although she did try and call me a few times, and message me, giving me the most pathetic excuse of all time. She said she thought it was Reid. "How fucking convenient," I mutter, making a scoffing sound at the thought. I had no idea about the issues Ryan had with his father. Of course, I knew their dad was an asshole, and was in prison, but I never knew anything else.

They didn't mention him and I didn't ask. Reid, Ryan and their younger brother, Reece, lived with their Auntie until they were eighteen and then moved out straight away. When we got married, I lived with the two of them in a small two-bedroom apartment. Things were tight, but they still worked for us. The three of us all worked and studied, working hard for a better future. Jack Kane, Summer's father, offered to give Reid and Ryan a loan to open the bar. The rest is history.

I don't know why Jack did that, other than the fact he used to be friends with their dad, and watched over them over the years after their mum died. I can't believe Ryan thinks those things about himself. He was a kid, no one would expect anything from him at that age. He should have been protected himself, not worrying about protecting others. It hurts to think of the childhood he had, but he and Reid have both turned out well, into men their mum would have been proud of. I park my car and get out, my mind still on Ryan. It comes down to two options. I either forgive him completely, or I don't. I either move on with my life with him in it, or without him. I can't live in limbo anymore. We both deserve much more than that.

I decide to take the stairs and take them two steps at a time, practically jogging to my apartment. As soon as I round the corner, I come to a standstill. Ryan is standing there, dressed to kill, in a crisp white shirt and black pants. His hair is slightly damp and pushed off his face, exposing his chiselled features and full lips. The most surprising part? He's on his knees, waiting for me.

"Ryan," I gasp, still in shock.

"The last time I proposed I couldn't afford the engagement ring you deserved, but this time I can," he says, his lips curving. He pulls out a black box and opens it so I can see. In the middle, sits the most beautiful ring I have ever seen. A solitary diamond, on a gold band. Simple and classic.

"Taiya Rose Knox, I have loved you ever since I knew what love was. I want to start over with you. I want to get to know you all over again, and I want to be with you for the rest of my life. Will you re-marry me?" he asks, staring up into my eyes with an expression that makes me melt. He looks hopeful, but also slightly unsure, like he has no idea what my response will be, but he's putting himself out there anyway.

"Ryan, stand up," I whisper, and by the crestfallen look on his face, he thinks that I'm rejecting him. I step up against him, aware that he's dressed up and smells like heaven and I'm in my dancing clothes. I go up on my tiptoes and kiss him smack on his mouth. "I'd love to start over with you," I tell him. His eyes light up and he lifts me into the air by my waist. He kisses me hungrily, sucking on my bottom lip before releasing me. Taking the ring out, he takes my hand and slides it onto the correct finger. The diamond is huge, and I know it cost him a fortune. Not that it matters to me. I would have been happy with the simple gold band he gave me the first time around.

"You look surprised," I state, giggling at his expression. Yes, giggling. I pull out my key so we don't have to stand here in front of my door all night, opening it for us to enter. Ryan locks the door behind us, standing behind me so close, I can feel the heat from his body, but not touching me. I inhale, not moving a muscle, waiting for him to touch me. I think I would die if he didn't. Slowly, he moves my hair off my shoulder, leaving my neck bare. He leans down and places one firm kiss on my neck, and a shiver runs down my spine at that one touch.

I clear my throat. "I'm going to have a shower. Be in my bed, naked," I say, tilting my head to take in his expression to my demand. His eyes are heavy lidded, and his lip curls up at the side. When he starts to undo his top button, I quickly head into the shower. Stripping down, I jump in without even testing the water, then squeal at its coldness.

"Are you okay?" comes a deep voice from outside the door.

"I'm fine!" I call out, adjusting the temperature. I grab my pink razor and quickly shave my legs, then put my apple scented body wash all over my body. I'm not going to lie. I'm a little nervous. I know Ryan's been with a lot of other women since we were last together, and as for me, I haven't been with anyone. Ryan is still the only man I've ever slept with, therefore I haven't had sex in a long-ass time. I will probably orgasm from him just looking at me. I groan, washing all the soap off my body. I quickly brush my teeth then turn the water off, grabbing my towel and wrapping it around myself. I stare at my reflection in the mirror, taking in my flushed cheeks, wild curly hair and towel-clad body.

It's time to take my man back.

CHAPTER FOURTEEN

Ryan

I sit on her bed, waiting for her. I don't think I've ever anticipated something this much. Okay, maybe back when we were sixteen and lost our virginity, but this sure as hell is a close second. I peel my shirt off and throw it onto the chair in the corner of her room. When she doesn't come out after five minutes after the water turns off, I walk to the bathroom and open the door without knocking. She's standing in front of the mirror, obviously over thinking things, like she usually does. She turns to look at me and gives me a nervous smile.

"I've already seen you completely naked, countless times, and now you're acting shy?" I ask her, unable to stop myself from chuckling. She spins around and narrows her eyes, suddenly letting the towel drop. There's my fiery Taiya. I don't want her thinking about anything other than us and our future. No more looking back, living in the past. As far as I'm concerned, none of those other women ever mattered or counted. I grab her hand and pull her into her bedroom, stopping for kisses along the way. Her breasts press up against my bare chest and I groan, loving the feel of her. There's nothing I want more than to shove her up against the wall and fuck her until we're both sated, but this is a new beginning for us, and I want to savour her. I grip her ass and squeeze, pulling her into me, as close together as physically possible.

"I love you," I tell her. I need her to know, to believe it.

"I love you, too," she says, before returning her lips to mine. She pulls away, dropping to her knees, and the sight of her is almost my undoing. She unbuckles my belt with haste, and pulls my pants and boxers down. Reaching her hand into my pants, she stokes my hardness, and my knees almost crumble. Nothing has ever felt better than her hands on me. Her delicate fingers circle the tip, before stroking my length over and over, until I'm unable to take anymore. I step back and pull my pants and boxers completely off, so we are both completely bare. I spin her around and push her down onto the bed, planning on tasting every inch of her amazing body.

"I need you inside me, Ryan," she rasps, her voice low and husky. I lean over her and kiss her greedily, while my fingers caress her intimately. She is dripping wet, and I'm hard as a fucking rock.

"Ryan!" she growls, when I trail my mouth down her neck. I bite down gently, and she lifts her hips, riding my fingers. I toy with her clit, which leaves her gasping for air. Before she comes, I pull my fingers out, and slide my cock into her. She mouths my name, and I curse. She feels so fucking good; it's like coming home. I pay attention to her breasts, licking and sucking, just how she used to like it. It only takes a few minutes for her to climax, her back arching off the bed and her fingers digging into my back. I watch her face, her expression. I don't know what it is about her; I just know that she was made for me. No other woman could ever replace Taiya Rose Knox, she owns me body and soul. I thrust into her quicker now, sliding right out before pushing myself in, balls deep. Taiya makes the sexiest little sounds, encouraging me to take more from her. She's always been a greedy little thing, and I wouldn't take her any other way. She lifts her hips up, moving in time with me. She captures my moan with her mouth as I release, my eyes closing as I feel nothing but pleasure coursing through my body.

"I missed you so much," I tell her, staring into those wide green eyes of hers.

She sighs, "I missed you more."

"Not possible, trust me. I felt like I was drowning without you." I slide out of her, and lay down next to her scooping her up in my arms. I absently play with her hair, gently pulling a curl and watching it spring up as I release it. I want to ask her how many men she's been with since she left, but I don't want to ruin the moment. I don't want us to get into a fight after how perfect tonight was. I'm still surprised she said yes. I knew it was a gamble, but after her avoiding me for another week since our talk, I was desperate. I didn't want to lose her, so I just put myself out there, hoping it would pay off and she would see just how much I love and need her. And now she's here in my arms, and mine again.

Everything is right in the world. Is it too soon to ask her to move in with me? Turning more to my side, I kiss her on her neck. "Will you move in with me?" I blurt out.

She turns her head to look at me, surprised. "Now?"

"Yes, why not?" I ask, frowning at her tone.

"What's the rush?"

"I just want you with me," I tell her, unable to explain it properly. I just had to have her close to me.

"Can we wait at least a month?" she says.

"You don't think this is going to work?"

"I didn't say that," she says, rubbing her thumb over my bottom lip. I pull it into my mouth and suck on it. She sucks in a breath. "Well… uhhh… Isis…"

"We will sort it out," I tell her, rolling her over so she's straddling me.

"Already?" she asks, breathless.

"I have over a year's worth of making up to do," I say, rubbing my thumb over her nipple.

"Is that right?" she purrs, lifting her head back.

"Yes. I need to see if you still like the same positions," She takes me into her hand and slides me into her, "If you still like me to wake you up with my mouth between your legs…" She groans and starts to ride me, hard and fast. I grip her hips and move with her, going as deep as I can.

This is going to be a long night, and we're both going to love every second of it.

*****

I wake up with a smile on my face, stretching my body lazily. Taiya is fast asleep on her stomach, her

102

hair pillowing around me. I place a kiss on the middle of her back, on her spine and then force myself out of bed. I don't think I've ever had so much sex in one night in my life, and that's saying something. I head into the kitchen, and pour some juice and put some bread in the toaster. I'd rung Isis yesterday and practically begged her to stay somewhere else for the night. She agreed, after I promised her a lot of free drinks at the bar. I would never expect her to pay anyway, but I didn't tell her that. I put some butter and vegemite on the toast and put in two more slices. I put Taiya's on a plate, cutting it in triangles like she used to have it every morning.

"You're making breakfast?" comes a sleepy voice. She walks out naked, not like we have anything to be shy about after last night. And this morning.

"How are you feeling?" I ask, putting the plate and juice in front of her.

"Hungry, tired and thoroughly fucked," she quips, making me laugh. "No, really. My legs feel shaky."

I grin, and Taiya laughs. "You should see your face. Full of satisfaction and male pride," she says around a bite of toast. I don't bother to deny it. I push her juice towards her, and she blesses me with a sweet smile. This is what I've missed out on. I know everything isn't solved between us but I'm more than willing to put in the work to get us to a happy place. We finish up in the kitchen then head into the shower.

"What's your plans for today?" Taiya asks as she gets dressed.

"I have to head into work, you?"

"I have a class to teach at three," she says, tying her hair up on top of her head.

"Okay, let's go out for lunch, and spend the day today together until you have to work."

"Sounds good."

"I'm gonna head home and get changed," I tell her, pointing down at my clothes from last night.

"Okay," she says smiling. "Maybe you should leave some of your clothes here, just in case."

I still. "Maybe I will."

"Good, now go and get dressed so you can feed your woman properly. Toast doesn't count," she says, leaving the room.

I smile so hard my cheeks hurt.

CHAPTER FIFTEEN

"Can you stop with the creepy smiling? You're scaring the customers," Jade announces. I couldn't stop smiling if I tried. After having an amazing meal with Taiya, she came back to my apartment and we hung out. She even reminded me just how talented that little mouth of hers was. I'm turned on just thinking about the image of her on her knees, so I try to think about something else.

Drinks. Taiya. What else do I have to do tonight? Taiya. Jade. Bingo. Semi hard on disappearing.

"What are you thinking about?" Jade asks nosily, leaning forward on the counter.

"I'm pretty sure that's pillow talk, Jade," I counter, staring down at the cash register.

"I wouldn't know since it's been that long since I got any," she mumbles, pushing her blonde hair behind her ear.

"Tag still doesn't want a piece, eh?" I ask, even though I already know the answer. Tag just isn't interested.

"No, and don't ask me when he got standards."

I laugh at that, to the point where one of the customers looks at me like I'm crazy.

"I'm assuming that cheesy grin is all about Taiya?"

"You'd be guessing right."

"Good. I'm happy for you," she says, slapping my shoulder, and then commences to pour a tequila shot.

"Who's that for?" I ask her just as she downs it. "Really, Jade?"

"What? I finish in an hour," she says, shrugging. Face meet palm. What did Reece see in her again?

I turn away from her, not about to allow her to ruin my great mood. "You can go home now."

"Cool," she says, clocking out and walking around to the other side of the bar. She plops down on the stool in front of me and grins. "Three tequilas please."

I stare at her for a second before I pour her one and slide it over to her. "That's all you're getting."

I'm saved from whatever smart ass remark she was going to throw my way when Tag walks in, early for his shift. Saved by the bald dude.

"Tag!" I say, louder than necessary, but I can't help it, Jade's mood swings are trying to bring me down.

"Happy to see me?" he asks, his eyes darting to Jade knowingly.

"Always," I say, grinning at him impishly.

He studies me for a second. "Someone got laid." I chuckle, but say nothing. I'm a gentleman after all. "You have this glow about you," he says in a mock high-pitched female voice, gesturing to his face in a circular motion.

"You worry me, Tag," I say through laughter. "Why are you here early? Just can't get enough of me, huh?"

He looks down, scowling. "Karen picked up Bella a little earlier, so I was sitting in the house doing nothing."

"Say no more," I say, putting my hands up. Tag hates sharing custody of his daughter.

"Do you want something to drink? Juice box?" I ask, pointing to Summer's stash.

"Don't mind if I do," he answers. I take out a juice box and throw it to him, turning to the counter to serve a customer. It starts to get busy, so Tag helps until the bar is cleared. Summer walks in an hour later, carrying her books.

"How was class?" I ask.

"Hectic. Did Reid drop by?" she asks, shoving her bag and books under the counter.

"He's still at the gym with Xander and Dash. Said he'd be here in an hour." Summer kisses Tag on the cheek and says hello to Jade. She takes me by the arm and pulls me into the office.

"How did it go?" she asks, her eyes sparking with excitement.

"Perfect, everything went perfect," I say, knowing I must look like a love sick puppy. I really couldn't care less.

"Yes!" she cheers, doing a little happy dance. She looks up at me, the biggest smile on her face. Almost as big as the one I've been wearing since the second I woke up. "I knew she wouldn't turn you down."

Well, I'm glad she had faith.

"When's she moving in?" And this is why Summer and I are friends.

"I think she wants to take it a little slower than that, but we'll see."

"You'll wear her down," she says confidently.

I sure as hell hope so.

*****

I pick up some dinner on the way home and go straight to Taiya's. Isis opens the door, wearing a robe, a towel wrapped around her hair.

"Hey stud," she says in greeting, opening the door for me to enter.

"Hey Isis. Thanks for last night," I cringe when I realise how that sounds. "For leaving the place so Taiya and I could be alone." I rang her up that morning to plan.

She nods. "No problem, anything to make Taiya happy."

I eye her. "And you were sure that would?"

She smiles knowingly. "She could deny it all she wanted. I knew she was crazy about you."

"Well, thank you all the same," I say, turning to Taiya's room.

Isis clears her throat. "In case you feel like you owe me, I know how you can repay."

I turn to look at her again, more warily this time. "What do you want?"

"Is Tag single?" she asks, trying to act nonchalant. Tag? Perhaps he should start a fan club.

"He's single, yes."

"Okay," she says, and turns to leave. Okay then. I walk to Taiya's door and open it, only to find it empty.

"Where's Taiya?" I call out, putting the food on the side table. Isis walks into the room, her damp red hair hanging down her shoulders.

"Oh, right. She went to see her mum. She should be home any minute."

"Okay, why didn't you tell me that?" I ask curiously.

"You didn't ask." Right, okay.

"I see," I answer slowly, drawing out the words.

"You don't, but you will," she says cryptically before walking away. I take my T-shirt off and jump into Taiya's bed.

When Taiya gets home, her face lights up as she spots me in her room watching TV. She throws her bag on the floor and jumps on top of me, before kissing me senseless.

"You look good in my bed," she says, laying her head on my chest.

"I brought dinner."

"I can see that, thank you," she murmurs. Her hands wander over my chest, leaving no spot untouched.

"What are you doing there, hmmmm?" I ask as her tongue peeps out to lick my abs.

"Showing my man how much I missed him today," she says softly. She sits up and lowers her head to kiss me, undoing my button at the same time. Taiya used to be very shy, and it's nice seeing her like this. Taking what she wants. Although it hurts to think of who she's been with to make her so comfortable. I push those thoughts away, instead concentrating on the pleasure my wife brings me. She pulls my cock out of my boxer shorts and takes me into her mouth with one long, deep suck.

This must be what heaven feels like.

CHAPTER SIXTEEN

I walk into Taiya's room without knocking, about to open my mouth to tell her about the plans I'd made for tonight. "What the fuck is that?" is what comes out, as soon as my eyes land on the bird sitting on her shoulder.

She smiles, and turns her face to the bird. "This is Leonardo, our new pet."

I stay silent.

"I told you I was getting a pet today, remember?"

"Yeah, I thought you were getting a puppy, or a fish, or something," I ramble, eyeing the bird.

"He's a cockatiel. Isn't he gorgeous?" she asks, cooing at the bird. Gorgeous. Not a word I'd use to describe a bird, but anyway. Taiya puts him back on his perch and stands.

"Give me a sec. I'll go and get his cage," she says, walking out of the room. Curious, I walk closer to the bird and put my hand out, the same way I saw Taiya doing. Instead of climbing on top of my hand, the little monster hisses and snaps at my fingers, trying to bite them.

"Vicious little thing, aren't you?" I mutter under my breath, eyeing Leonardo with distaste. When he

111

hisses again, I step away. Taiya steps back into the room with a cage, putting it on the floor in the corner of her room.

"He isn't going to sleep in here, is he?" I ask her, dreading the answer.

"No," she answers, laughing. "I'm going to put him in the front room." Well, thank fuck for that.

"I have something planned for us tonight," I tell her, wrapping my hands around her tiny waist. She puts the bird into the cage and spins around, giving me her full attention.

"What are you up to?" she asks suspiciously, leaning her head on my chest.

"Can't a man spoil his wife?" I say, kissing her on top of her head. I love having her in my arms. It feels like everything is right in the world. Like I'm right where I'm meant to be. The last two weeks, since I gave her the ring, have been like a honeymoon. Taiya and I, together every day. Making love, going out for romantic dates, getting to know each other again. It's been the best time of my life. She is perfect. Perfect for me.

"I'm pretty sure you've been spoiling me for a while now," she says, looking up at me. I push an errant curl away from her face.

"You better get used to it," I tell her, running my fingers down her soft cheek.

"I have to admit something," she says, looking a little sheepish.

"What's that?"

"I moved into this building because I knew you were here, and even if I was mad at you, I wanted to be near you," she says, rushing out the words.

I smile widely. "I knew it!"

"You did not," she says, rolling her eyes.

"Okay, I didn't. I couldn't believe how lucky I was. Summer said she mentioned the place to you."

She nods. "She did, and she also mentioned that you lived here too."

Summer failed to tell me that part. "That was a gamble," I mutter.

"A gamble that paid off, clearly."

"You're right. And I'm so fucking happy with the way everything turned out. Now, I get to touch you whenever I want," I say as my hands grip her ass.

"You have it bad, Ryan," Taiya jokes, leaning up to kiss me on the jawline. Fuck, she's sweet. I'm about to show her just how sweet she is when my phone rings, blasting that stupid fox song. Taiya starts laughing, and I know then that it's her who put it there. I tickle her under her breast, before answering.

Then I head straight to Reid's to find out what the hell is going on.

*****

Reid stands by the window in his bedroom, staring outside. He has a blank look on his face, and I know straight away something is wrong. He said nothing on the phone, just for me to come over because he needed to talk to me about something. Summer and Taiya are in the kitchen, giving Reid and me some space to talk alone. I love that the two of them

113

understand that sometimes Reid and I just need to be there for each other. It may sound girly, or whatever, but being a twin means I'm connected to him in a way no one might ever understand. And I wouldn't expect them to.

"What's going on?" I ask, sitting on the edge of his bed. He picks up a piece of paper and hands it to me without saying a word. It's a letter. From our father. I glance up at Reid and he nods his head encouragingly. I read over the letter, once, twice. "Are you fucking kidding me?" I growl, putting the paper on the bed and standing up. Reid scrubs his hand over his face, and then looks me dead in the eye.

"We need to find her," is all he says.

I nod, smiling bitterly. "We will."

I have a half-sister I had no idea about. And only now he wants to tell us, just spring it on us like this. In a fucking letter. Is she okay? Is she living a good life? Does she know about us? Did our mum know that he cheated on her? So many unanswered questions, and since I'm not going to go to the source to ask for answers, I'm just going to have to try and find them out for myself. Starting with her. Persephone Knox.

I put my hand on Reid's shoulder, squeezing. "We have a baby sister, huh!"

He smirks a little. "I feel sorry for her already."

"Tell me about it. So this is how Xander felt," I say, and we both go quiet, lost in our own thoughts.

"What if she doesn't want anything to do with us?" he asks suddenly, sitting down on the bed.

"We will worry about that when we get to it. First we need to find her."

He tightens his lips. "We could have had her in our lives this whole time. Even if it was just on holidays. We would have kept an eye on her, make sure she wanted for nothing. He is such a selfish fuck."

I nod. "I know." What else is there to say? Our father is a dickhead; there's really nothing new there. I have to wonder why he decided to tell us. Probably for us to come and see him to beg for her whereabouts. Maybe he needs money or something.

"How do we know he isn't lying?" I ask. Reid stands and gets the envelope on the table. He hands it over to me, and I peep inside. Pulling out the small photo, I stare at it. It's my father, another woman, and a little baby girl. She's blonde, and cute. I turn the photo over, and it reads 'Persephone'.

I swallow hard, taking in every detail on the photograph. I don't know why it hurts, but it does. He had a whole other family. Is that why he hated us so much?

"Stay in the present, Ry," Reid says, pulling me from my thoughts.

I go rigid. "It's a little more complicated than that, isn't it?"

"Yes, but we need to think about Seph now," he says, rubbing the back of his neck.

I pause. "You've already given her a nickname?" I ask, my lips twitching.

"That name is a little long," he pauses, "and ridiculous."

I nod in agreement. "She needs an R name."

He laughs. "That's exactly it."

"You know, I think we're going to be amazing brothers."

I flash him a look that says 'well, duh.' "So I guess we start with the internet."

"We should ask Mia to help," he says, surprising the shit out of me.

"What?" I ask, confused.

"She's like the FBI. I remember when we were dating, she would hack into everything, my phone, my email, and track me down at random times." We both laugh, and I know he's only messing around, trying to lighten up the situation.

"Yeah, it's funny now," he says, clearing his throat. I laugh harder at the expression on his face.

"Come on, let's go talk with our women," he says, making me grin.

"Now who's whipped?"

"Still you," I reply.

He scoffs. "Well, yes, but now you can't judge me for it."

"Fine, we'll call it even."

"Equally pussy whipped?"

I still. "Well, yes. But you don't admit that." At least not out loud. Or in public.

"Pussy whipped but can't admit it, got it," he says, his smile letting me know he's just being a tool.

"You worry me sometimes."

"You love me."

I do. "All right, let's call in the reinforcements. Tomorrow, we start looking for Persephone."

CHAPTER SEVENTEEN

Taiya

When we get back to Ryan's apartment, his mood has suddenly changed. He is quiet and almost zoned out. I know that he was just processing the news of his sister, so I let him have his space. I know how much Ryan values family, even though his dad is an asshole; he loves Reid with everything he has. He is so loving, always trying to take care of everyone around him. He even offered Isis a job when she mentioned looking for something to make some extra cash. Ryan is always willing to help someone else. That's just who he is. Knowing he has a sister out there, I can't imagine how he's feeling. Her being a half-sister doesn't matter to him; I know that. Ryan wants her in his life, and he's going to make sure it happens. Almost like he did with me. I hope we're able to locate her soon, and that she is happy and well.

I fill up the bathtub, undress and get in. The warm water feels amazing, and I let my head fall back, feeling relaxed after what turned out to be a stressfully eventful evening. An hour later, I'm in my robe and walking towards the bedroom, when I hear banging. I rush into the games room, where Ryan is beating the shit out of a punching bag, barehanded.

"Ryan…"

He cuts in. "I'm not good company right now, Tay." I think it's just hit him. His father. His sister. I wonder if I should leave him alone, or if he needs me right now. He punches the bag a few more times, and then turns to face me.

"Go to bed," he says, before ignoring me.

"I'll wait for you," I tell him, not backing down. He stops and his body goes rigid. He then turns, walking towards me.

"You don't want to be around me right now," he says. His knuckles are red but not split, and there is sweat tricking down his bare chest. I take a step, so we're so close that we're almost touching.

"Don't push me away, Ry," I say, putting my hand on his arm.

He stares at it for a second before replying. "I'm not pushing you away I just need—"

I cut in, "I know what you need."

"You don't want me to fuck you right now," he says, turning his back on me and walking back to the centre of the room. Bristling a little at his rejection, I head back into his bedroom and take my robe off, getting under the sheets. Since it doesn't look like I'll be getting any action tonight, I decide to take care of it myself. I stroke my fingers over my nipples, then trailing them down over my stomach, past my belly button and…

"What are you doing?" he asks in a tone that lets me know he knows *exactly* what I was doing.

I pull the sheet up to my chin. "Nothing," I lie. He rips the sheet off me, his eyes raking over my naked body.

"You sure you want me right now?" he says, his eyes still on my body.

I shiver. "Yes."

As soon as the word leaves my mouth, he's on me, kissing my lips roughly and tangling his hands in my hair. His body is still damp with perspiration, and I moan at the friction of his body against my nipples. He smells so good, all Ryan, cologne and sweat. He pulls his mouth away, straddling my hips without putting any weight on my body. He lifts a finger to his mouth, sucking on it before reaching his hand back and gently stroking me. I mouth the word 'fuck' as he slides a thick finger inside me. He's still wearing his basketball shorts, and I need him to take them off. Now. I lift my hands up, sticking my thumbs into each side of his waistband, and slowly lower them. My gaze hungrily takes in my favourite part on a man, the sexy V that points to something I wouldn't mind having my mouth wrapped around right now...

I look up into his eyes, darker than usual, and see him smirk. He moves off me and rolls me over onto my stomach. I hear him take off his shorts, then lean over me and kiss me on my neck. He pulls my hair aside and trails kisses down my neck, and all the way down my spine. I beg for him to give me more, but he takes his time with me, until I lose my patience. I lift myself up on my knees and push back against him, hoping he can take a damn hint. When I feel his tongue suddenly on me, I call out his name, fisting the sheets with white knuckles. His tongue leaves me, and

I sigh in disappointment, until he slides into me, thrusting hard, the headboard banging with each movement.

I push back against him, loving the feel of him. He puts his hand on the back of my neck, gently holding me in place. He reaches down between us and toys with my clit, pushing me over the edge. I bite down on the pillow as I reach my peak, my thighs quaking. Ryan quickens his speed, and I know he's now concentrating on himself, on getting him to where I've just been. I turn my head to look at him. When he sees my eyes on him he leans down and kisses me, long hard and wet.

"I love you," he tells me as he finishes, slamming into me for the last time.

"Love you, too," I mumble, feeling tired and sleepy, and so fucking relaxed and satisfied. He pulls out of me, and spoons me from behind.

"Why do you put up with me?" he asks. Ryan rarely gets moody. Unless he's jealous, or feeling some other caveman tendency, he is generally easy going, quick to joke and playful. When he does get into a mood where he snaps at me, he usually feels bad afterwards, and is always sure to make up for it. While Reid is generally broody all the time, Ryan has a temper that hardly comes out, but when it does, people better run.

"For the sex," I reply, earning me a playful bite on my shoulder. "Okay fine, you also bring me food all the time. That's a really good quality in a man."

I kiss him on the back of his hand. "Because, Ryan Knox, I always knew you were going to be mine. I'll never love anyone how I love you, and because you have a really huge–" He cuts me off by turning my face and kissing me.

*****

After trying all different kinds of social networks and coming up with nothing, we decide to ask Summer's dad for help. Apparently, he has all kinds of badass connections, plus since he used to be friends with Ryan's dad, maybe he knew something about her. Anything at all. Jack Kane is a scary looking man, with tattoos and a beard. He looks like a biker, but he has kind eyes and a nice laugh.

"Now what?" I ask Ryan as we leave Jack's house. Jack had no idea about Persephone. In fact, he seemed as shocked as we were. I take his hand as he leads me to his bike.

"Now, beautiful, you are going to teach your class and I'm going to the bar."

I look at my watch. "Fuck."

Ryan laughs. "Yes, we better hurry our asses."

I pause at his bike. "How are you feeling?"

"Surprisingly optimistic, actually," he says, tugging on a curl of hair. "I think you might have something to do with that."

"Me?"

"Yes, you."

"What did I do?" I ask, wrapping my arms around him.

"Well, you're here for one," he says, his eyes soft.

He's so damn sweet. "Can we fit in a quickie before work?"

Ryan laughs. "Look what I've created. Or were you like this before we got back together?" he says, his look turning dark. Ahh, the huge elephant in the room. I haven't told Ryan yet that I haven't been with anyone else. It makes me look kind of pathetic, but at the same time I guess it's a little romantic.

Who am I kidding, it's definitely pathetic.

"Well... uhh... you see," I ramble, feeling a little awkward.

His jaw ticks. "Let's go," he says, turning his back on me and putting on his helmet. I do the same, sighing and getting on behind him.

We get home and he walks me to my door. "Will you come to the bar tonight to see me?" he asks.

I nod, "Sure, I'll be there around nine with Isis."

"Okay," he says leaning down to give me a quick kiss. "Look about before, I'm sorry. I have no reason to be angry, considering... fuck. I'm sorry. I love you."

"I love you too, but, Ryan—"

He cuts me off, "You don't have to explain." He gives me a small smile and then walks away.

*****

Isis giggles and smooths down her dress. Pre-drinks were not a good idea. I only had one drink, but Isis decided four was a nice even number.

"Tag is going to love me in this dress," she says, beaming.

I laugh. "Have you even seen him since that night?"

"Well, no. But the chemistry was undeniable."

"So is that what those drinks were about? Liquid courage?" I ask, crossing the road to the bar.

She hiccups. "I guess so." I don't think Tag is going to be turned on if she's sloppy drunk, so I hope she sobers up a little before trying to approach him.

"How do I look?" she asks. She's wearing a white dress; this one strapless and peplum. With all her beautiful red hair, she kind of looks like Ariel from *'The Little Mermaid.'*

"Beautiful."

"Thank you. You look hot too. You're totes, a babe," she says, nodding appreciatively as she gives me a once over. Great, drunk Isis says 'totes.' We walk to the bar's entrance arm in arm, and instantly hear the music and laughter. The place is pretty packed tonight. I can't help but feel a sense of pride as I walk in. Ryan has really done well for himself. Ryan, Tag and Reid are all serving customers, and I instantly know why the bar is filled with women. Reid is wearing a black T-shirt, and Ryan is wearing white. Apart from Reid's scar and their different hairstyles, you can't tell them apart. Tag is wearing a tight white singlet, showing off his muscles. This is like the male version of fucking Hooters. I try to tone down the jealousy, but as I look around and wonder which one of these girls Ryan has been with, I start to grind my teeth. Ryan spots me and smiles, biting his bottom lip as he sees what I'm wearing. High waisted denim shorts and a black crop top, showing about two inches of my stomach. Paired with red platform heels, I think I clean up pretty well.

"I want to run my hands over that bald head," Isis says into my ear. I scrunch up my face at that visual, and head to the bar as I see Ryan walk towards me.

"Look at you," he says, pulling me into his arms and kissing me. "What do you want to drink?"

"Juice for me and I think Isis needs a water," I tell him, looking behind me at Isis who is blowing Tag a flying kiss. Get some game woman! Ryan chuckles and leads me to the stool right in front of where he was standing. He lifts me onto the chair, giving me a look so heated, I forget all about my jealousy and insecurities.

"You take my breath away," he says so only I can hear. "I'm going to fuck you in those heels tonight."

I blush. Ryan leads Isis to her seat and helps her up; he says something to her before getting back behind the bar. Reid and Tag both say hello, and Ryan gets us our drinks. I don't bother trying to pay because last time Ryan made a scene over it when I told him I wanted to. He went all dramatic and told me that this bar was mine, and if I wanted cash, I could take it from the cash register. He then opened said register and asked me how much I wanted. I want to kill him all over again at the memory.

Isis looks at the bottle of water and then narrows her eyes. "Water? Really?"

I shrug. She isn't slurring her words so she can't be too drunk, but I'd rather be safe than sorry.

"One water, then one drink," she says, nodding her head like we made a deal.

I grin. "Are you bartering with me?"

"It's called compromise, and… wait what was I talking about? Oh, hi Tag," she says, leaning on her palm.

"Isis," he says, smiling. "Taiya, looking gorgeous I see."

"Always," I answer, winking at him. He chuckles and looks behind us, asking if anyone is waiting to be served. I look for Ryan, and frown when I see him at the opposite side of the bar talking to a woman. He's shaking his head no at her, while she leans closer to say something to him. Who exactly is that? It could just be a friend. Men have women friends all the time, right? When she reaches up her hand to touch his jaw, I have my answer. Ryan looks over at me, as if checking to see if I saw that, grimacing when he realises I did. The woman follows his line of direction and her lips tighten. She walks away, and I see Ryan rub the back of his neck, as if steeling himself before having to deal with me. I look away and down into my juice, moving the ice cubes around with the straw.

"Tay," he says, wrapping me in his arms from behind.

"Who was that?" I ask, not beating around the bush.

He sighs, like he knew the interrogation was coming. "Someone I used to know."

"Right, and I get that, Ryan, but why was she touching you now?"

"She didn't know I was taken." Then he mutters under his breath, "And she didn't believe me when I told her I was."

I nod. "Why would they believe you, right? I mean you've been every woman's go-to-cock for the last year."

He flinches at my comment, gripping the bridge of his nose. "It's going to happen, beautiful, and each time I'm going to tell them I'm not interested."

That mollifies me somewhat, and I know I may be overreacting, but it still hurts. "Stupid whore," I mutter under my breath.

"She's not a whore just because she slept with me, babe. Don't be like that," he says, sounding disappointed. Disappointed! In me!

"Are you sticking up for her?" I ask, my mouth gaping.

"No, but it's not her fault, is it? I'm the one in the wrong, not her."

You know how in books, the man usually sleeps around a lot and doesn't really care or respect anyone's feelings, but when he meets *the* woman he changes instantly, treating her like a queen because she's different and not skanky. Why couldn't Ryan be like that! My rational side knows that Ryan respects all women. He doesn't judge them or treat them badly. I should be happy about that, be proud that this man is mine. But right now, all I can see is him sticking up for a woman who had her hands on his face, and has had his dick in her body. I see red.

"I see," I say, drawing out each word.

Ryan scrubs his hands over his face, probably wondering what exactly I'm seeing and what it means for him.

"You've been married to me this whole time, and it didn't stop you then, did it. You're acting like we only just got married."

I see the first flash of anger in his eyes. "Well, you're the one who left me that letter. What did it say in it again? Oh, that's right," he says, dramatically drawing out the syllables of the last three words, "'Move on without me, because I'll be doing the same.' You can't throw it in my face now, Tay. That's really not fair. If you didn't leave me that letter, you think I would have ever touched another woman?"

His question hangs heavily in the air between us. The taste of regret is thick and bitter. Isis sticks her head in, frowning. "You okay, Taiya?" she asks, narrowing her pale blue eyes on Ryan.

"I'm fine," I tell her, forcing a smile. The bar gets crowded and Ryan leaves to help out.

"What was that about?" she asks, downing the last of her water.

I swallow hard, watching him. "Nothing," I say, not wanting to ruin her night with my problems. "Shall we get a drink?"

"A real drink?"

I laugh. "Yes, a real drink."

"Okay, I'll get us something," she says, a little too cheerfully if you ask me. She walks straight up to Tag, almost pushing some other woman out of the way. Ryan's words replay in my mind. Why did I leave that stupid letter? I was hurt, that's why. I was devastated, and trying to save face. I told him in the letter to consider us separated, and to move on because I wasn't his anymore. I wrote it just after I saw him with her, and left it for him, covered in my tears. I can put the blame on him all I want, but the truth is that I messed up too. I shouldn't have left, shouldn't have left that letter. I know there's no point in looking back, wondering what if. How do we move forward though? The past isn't always so easy to forget, because it's moulded us into who we are today.

"Here you go," Isis says, handing me a tequila shot. With no lime or salt. Great.

"Tequila? Are you sur—"

She cuts me off, "Cheers!"

She swallows hers in one gulp, while I'm still staring at mine. Oh, what the hell. I tilt my head back, letting the alcohol slide down my throat, and then slam the shot glass down on the table. I can feel Ryan's eyes on me, but I don't look up at him. I'm still raw from our conversation. Isis saves me by grabbing my hand and pulling me towards the dance floor. Or at least the bar's version of one.

A few songs later, Ryan grabs me from behind and spins me around. "All the men are watching you," he growls, his jaw ticking.

I glance around, and it's true; a few men's eyes are on me. The thing is, I'm a dancer. I live to dance. I don't dance for other people. I dance for me. So I don't really care who's watching, I just enjoy myself, getting lost in the music and the rhythm.

"So what?" I say. Not like I'm interested or going home with any of them.

He apparently doesn't like my answer. "I don't like them seeing you like this."

"Like what?" I ask.

He leans down and speaks into my ear. "You look so fucking sexy, dancing like this. You look so free. I don't like them seeing you."

I bite the inside of my cheek. "So what? You want me to sit in the corner and do nothing?" I'm having déjà vu right now. Ryan and I have had this fight before. I remember when I used to perform at high school concerts and he used to complain about the whole school seeing my 'moves.' He's ridiculous. I tell him so. Isis pulls him to dance, and I laugh as he awkwardly tries to move away from her. She pulls him back and starts doing a half-grinding half-thrusting move, and he stares at me with a 'please help me' look. I grin, and walk back to the bar, leaving him to his own devices. I sit in front of Tag, who is watching Ryan and laughing.

"Threw him to the wolves, did you?" he asks, a humorous glint in his eyes.

I raise an eyebrow. "Are you calling my best friend a she wolf?"

He grins. "She's beautiful…"

"But?"

"But… I'm not really looking for something right now. I haven't even been with a woman in a few weeks, and I'm usually the one who…" He looks at me, realising who he's talking to and clears his throat. "Well, let's just say I made Ryan look like a choir boy."

"Nice," I say dryly.

He winces. "I'm sorry, for what it's worth he never even thought about getting serious with anyone after you left. It was you or no one."

"By no one, you mean endless bouts of meaningless sex?"

He pours me a juice and slides it over. "He was trying to forget you. It was his coping mechanism. I'm sure you did what you had to do to try and get over him, to try and move on with your life."

I sip on the juice, not saying anything. "He's a good man," Tag says, not taking his eyes off me.

"I know," I tell him.

"Don't hurt him, Taiya," Tag says softly, his baldhead cocked to the side.

"He's the one who fucked up and hurt me," I say, turning to watch him dance with Isis.

"I think he's paid his price, haven't you?" he says, before leaving to serve someone.

"Are you okay?" Reid asks. I turn to face him and smile.

"I'm fine. Where's Summer?" I ask him, moving the subject away from me. He gives me a look that says he knows what I'm doing, but answers me anyway.

"She's at her brother's house."

I'm about to reply when Ryan comes up behind me and wraps his arms around me.

"Let's go home."

"Now?" I ask, looking around for Isis.

"Yes, Reid is taking Isis home. She wants to stay a little longer."

I stand up. "Okay." I say bye to Isis, Tag and Reid. Ryan practically pulls me out of the bar.

"What's the rush?" I ask.

"Need to be inside you."

"Oh."

"Yes, oh."

He starts his bike and I hold on tight.

CHAPTER EIGHTEEN

Taiya

"I wasn't with anyone while I was gone," I blurt out. I run my fingers over his stomach, not looking at him. I feel him go rigid, and he puts his hand on mine, stopping my fidgeting.

"You weren't?" he asks, his voice husky.

"No."

He clears his throat. "Why not?"

"What do you mean 'why not'?"

"Say it, Taiya," he demands, cupping my face and lifting my chin up to look at him.

"Because I didn't... I don't want anyone else."

He looks at me in such a way that I actually feel lightheaded. "I love you."

"You damn well better."

He smiles with his eyes. "I'm never letting you go again. You know that, right?"

"As long as you treat me how I deserve to be treated, I don't think that's going to be a problem," I say, placing a kiss on his chin.

He rolls over so I'm under him and kisses me. "I'll always treat you like a princess. Well, maybe not in the bedroom," he adds. I pinch his ass, making him laugh. His phone rings, and as he gets up to answer it, I head to the bathroom to have a shower. When I come out, dressed for the day, Ryan is sitting on the edge of the bed in his boxer shorts staring down at his phone.

"What is it?" I ask, standing before him.

"Jack wants Reid and me to go and see him."

"He found her?" I ask, running my palm down the back of his head.

"He didn't say. He just said to go and see him," he says, looking up at me.

"Cryptic much?" I say as I move my fingers along the stubble across his jaw. "Are you going now?"

"Yes. As soon as my wife kisses me, I'll have a quick shower and go," he says, nuzzling my tummy. I straddle his lap and give him a kiss he will be thinking about all day. My hands start to roam and he pulls back, his heavy lidded eyes staring into mine. "Those lips are magic."

"I must have had a good teacher," I say, wiggling my eyebrows.

"Damn straight," he says, rubbing his hands down my thighs.

"Lots of practice on your end? Hmmmm," I tease, grinning at his slightly sheepish look at my dig at his experience.

"Are you ever going to let that go?" he asks, his voice turning serious.

I bite my bottom lip. "I'll try. I get jealous and that's kind of hard to control."

He grins at that. "Trust me, I know the feeling."

"You've never had to share me with anyone. How could you possibly know the feeling?"

He scowls. "Just the thought is bad enough." I kiss him again, before he heads for a shower and I head back to my apartment.

*****

I walk into my apartment, grinning when I see Isis in the kitchen, looking like death. "What happened to you last night?" I ask her.

She jumps in the air, obviously not hearing me enter and grimaces. "I'd rather not talk about it."

I laugh. "No really what happened?" I walk and sit down on the chair, all ears.

"A lot of dancing, more drinks. A conversation with Tag," she says, her face in her palm.

"I asked him if he wanted to go home with me," she says, her eyes wide with horror and embarrassment.

"And?" I ask.

"And... he said no, because I was drunk," she says, putting two painkillers in her mouth and swallowing them down with some iced water. "Reid took me home. Where I threw up. Twice."

I look around the house, like I'm going to see evidence.

"In the bathroom," she adds dryly.

"Well, at least that's something," I say, trying to contain my laughter.

"Very funny! I'm going back to bed."

"No work today?"

"No I called in sick," she says, heading into her room. I grab my handbag and head to my mum's house. I usually help her clean her house, and do grocery shopping so she doesn't have extra things to worry about during the week. She's also been dying to know the latest about me and Ryan. She's loved Ryan from day one and hated it when we separated. I call out bye to Isis and head out.

*****

That night, Ryan and I have dinner together at my favourite restaurant. Jack had given them the last known address of twenty-two-year-old Persephone Knox. With a name like that, Jack found her easily enough, located at an address about thirty minutes from here. Ryan and Reid are heading there tomorrow, first thing in the morning. I hope everything goes well for the two of them.

"Why are we stopping here?" I ask when Ryan stops off at the bar, on the way home.

"Need to pick something up from the office," he says. "Come in for a second? I don't want you sitting here alone."

I nod and get out of the car. Ryan holds my hand as we enter, and leaves me at the bar with Tag, while he heads out the back.

"Hello gorgeous," Tag says, putting his elbows on the bar.

"Hey you. Heard last night was eventful," I say, smiling widely.

He groans. "She's beautiful, she is." Is all he says about his rejection of Isis. My mouth gapes open as I see a woman walk into Ryan's office.

"Who the fuck was that?" I ask, standing up. I almost want to tie my hair up and take out my earrings.

"Who?" Tag asks.

"Never mind," I mumble, walking to the office and opening the door. I see Ryan at his desk, and the mystery woman standing in front of him. Ryan stands when he sees me, giving me an apologetic look.

"Tay, come here beautiful," he says, opening his arms to me. I walk over to him and he wraps me in his arms. "This is my wife," he says to the pretty brunette. She narrows her eyes on me before turning and storming away.

"And don't come into the office again please," Ryan calls out, sighing drearily.

"Past conquest?" I gather.

"I don't know what I was thinking. Fucking where I work! I'm sorry…"

"Don't bother," I say, an idea forming.

"Don't get mad, Tay," he says, his grip on me tightening.

"There's a new rule. Every time one of your ex-girlfriends comes up to us and ruins my night, you have to go down on me for an hour," I say.

Ryan's smile turns devilish. "How's that a punishment?"

"I don't return the favour. In any way," I say, inwardly grinning at the look on his face.

He scowls, brows drawing together. "Nothing at all?"

"Nothing," I say, trying not to look smug and failing.

He scoffs, "As if you can go without me inside you."

That is the truth. "I think I'll manage. It won't be every night we run into your exes." Or at least I hope.

"They aren't my exes," he snaps, brows drawing together.

"Whatever." Exes or not, they still had him.

"This torture starts from the next time though, right?" he asks hopefully. He sticks out his bottom lip in a pout and I want to suck on it.

"No," I say smiling up at him innocently and batting my eyelashes. I kiss him on his mouth and then walk out of the office, back to chat with Tag.

CHAPTER NINETEEN

Ryan

Reid and I stare at the shabby looking building and cringe.

"She lives here?" Reid growls, looking around the not-so-nice neighbourhood. The surrounding houses are old and not so well kept, with brown grass covered in rubbish. The building itself doesn't look so bad, except for a few broken windows I can see from here.

"Not for long," I add, trying to calm my nerves. We walk into the building, and take the stairs to the third floor. The elevator is out of order. Knocking on the door, I wait a few seconds before knocking again. The door swings open, and there she stands. Our baby sister. Shoulder-length blonde hair, warm brown eyes and a small petite body. She looks so cute, like a little angel. And then she opened her mouth.

"Who the fuck are you?" she asks rudely, her head looking from me to Reid multiple times.

I open and close my mouth, looking at Reid for help. "We need to talk," Reid says.

"Do I need to get my gun?" Persephone asks, sounding bored. She even glances down and inspects her fingernails.

"You don't have a gun," I tell her. At least, I hope she doesn't.

"I could have a gun," she says, a little defensively.

"Are you Persephone Knox?" I ask, wanting to make sure it really is her.

"What's it to you?" she asks, her eyebrows drawing together suspiciously.

"We just want to talk," I say, trying to smile to make her feel more comfortable.

"Look, I get that I'm the hottest chick in the building, but I'm not into," she waves her hand around animatedly, "whatever double teaming shit you've got going on over here."

Reid makes a choking noise and I scrub my hand down my face. So many things wrong with that statement.

"What?" she shrugs. "I read, a lot. I know what people are into these days."

Okaaaay. This is awkward as fuck. "No, we are actually here for the opposite of whatever it is you're thinking about now?" I ramble.

Her face takes on a thoughtful expression. "You want to go rescue animals with me?"

What the fuck. "How is that the opposite of sex?"

She smirks. "Sounds pretty fucking opposite to me." It's official. My sister is weird.

Reid cuts into our weird and slightly disturbing conversation. "We're here about your father."

"My dad's a deadbeat," she says, fidgeting with the sleeves of her white top. Her expression falters a little but she tries to quickly mask it.

"We know. He's also our father," I add in softly. There is a beat of silence.

She looks interested, but still a little unsure. "Prove it." Reid pulls out his driver's licence and shows it to her. She looks at us both. I mean really looks at us, and then opens the door wide. We walk in and take a seat on a new looking pink couch. She sits opposite us and sighs. "Start from the beginning."

And we do. We tell her everything up until we received the letter.

"So I have elder twin brothers," she says, her lips curving.

"I guess you do," Reid says, smiling a little.

"So tell us about you," I say, eager to know more.

She lifts her shoulder in a shrug. "Haven't seen Dad since I was a kid. My mum died a few years ago. I'm a uni student, studying law. I work part time at a café. That's about it."

Even though I had nothing to do with it, I can't help but feel proud. She's studying and working, making something of herself. "Good," Reid says softly, and I know he feels what I'm feeling right now.

"So start packing your shit and get ready to go," Reid tries to say casually but fails.

I groan, pinching the bridge of my nose.

"What the hell are you on about?" she asks, sitting up straighter.

"What Reid is trying to say is you can come live with us. I have plenty of room, and we own a bar you could work in, and we want to take care of you and make up for lost time," I try to explain.

"Yeah, I don't think so," she says, standing up. The universal gesture for 'time to go.' "I'm happy to have met you guys, and I would love to get to know the two of you and have you in my life, but I'm not moving."

"But…" Reid starts, until he sees the stubborn look on Persephone's face.

She grins. "I get that you are clearly both used to getting your way, but not this time."

"Okay, will you let us take you out for lunch now?" I ask, not wanting to leave her just yet.

"Sure, I'd like that," she says, smiling. "Only if I get to choose the place."

"Deal," Reid and I say at the same time, sharing a relieved look, and then taking our baby sister out to lunch.

*****

"We have to get some real food," I say after we drop Persephone off at home.

"Agreed, seriously. I think she took us to that place on purpose," Reid says, staring at the road.

"I know she did," I grumble. Her eyes were alight with mischief as she watched us order from a menu of rabbit food. "She's probably not even vegetarian." Reid grunts in agreement. We glance at each other, and both start chuckling. She's something, that girl.

"I feel like a weight's been lifted," I tell my brother. "I wish she'd move in with us. Hell, we could try to get her an apartment here in the building."

"We'll wear her down eventually," he says with confidence.

I'm not so sure. "Stubborn seems to be her middle name."

"Why do you think he sent us to her?" Reid asks suddenly.

I shrug. "Maybe because she has no other family." From what Persephone told us, it was just her and her mother. She isn't close and doesn't keep in contact with anyone from her mum's side. So it looks like we're it for her.

"Maybe he felt guilty," I say, looking out the window. Maybe, just maybe, he felt a little remorse for all the things he's done over the years. At least now, we can look after Sephie so she's not alone.

"As he should," Reid growls, clearly not wanting to discuss our father.

"I'm fucking exhausted," I say, changing the subject. "Are you going to the gym or home?"

"Summer's meeting me at the gym," he says, turning onto the main road. "You want me to drop you off at home or at the bar?"

"Bar."

"I'm really happy you and Taiya sorted your shit out," Reid says.

"Me too," I breathe. More than anyone could fucking imagine.

"So you're solid?"

"Yeah, we're solid."

"Good," he says quietly. "Everything's still on then?"

"Yep," I answer.

Reid drops me off, and I head into the bar, grinning when I see a familiar face. "About time you came out to play," I tell Dash, taking a seat next to him.

"Trust me, after the month I've had, I deserve some time to relax," he says, twirling his glass before taking a sip.

"What do you want, boss?" Jade asks, looking a little bored.

"Nothing for me, thanks, Jade," I say, turning my attention back to Dash. "Anything I can do for you, my man?"

He tightens his lips. "No, but thanks for the offer."

Dash is a proud man. He won't ask or accept any help. "This about your sisters? You know we can always watch the younger ones for you."

His violet eyes find mine. "It's not the younger ones who are causing trouble. I hope I never have any daughters; that's all I'm saying."

"How old is the trouble maker?" I ask him.

"Fifteen. I'm the only one she listens to, so I'm trying to be at home as much as possible." Dash looks tired, and worn out.

"Let me know if we can help. I'm sure Taiya and Summer will be happy to keep her occupied."

"That's actually a good idea, thanks."

"No problem."

"I heard about you and Taiya. About fucking time, man," he says, smirking.

"Thanks and I couldn't agree more," I say, looking around the bar, taking in the customers. A few of the usuals and a few newbies. "Come by and see us if you're around. Hell, bring the tribe with you."

Dash nods, like he's considering it. "All right."

"You need to get your mind off things?" I ask, nodding towards two women at one of the tables. Awkward when I realise I've actually been with one of those two women.

Dash laughs. "No thanks. Your sloppy seconds don't sound very enticing," he says, brushing off my offer. I can't remember the last time I saw Dash with a woman. I know he was interested in Summer, but I don't think he's been interested in anyone else since.

"How do you know it's my sloppy seconds?" I ask, frowning.

Dash chuckles, downing the rest of his drink before answering. "You should call this place Knox's pussy."

I cringe, glad Taiya isn't here to hear that. "Nice, real nice, Dash," I mutter, running my hands down my face.

"It's the truth," he says, smiling and showing off those twin dimples I hear women swooning about.

"It's the past," I counter, standing up and walking behind the bar. "How's work?" Dash is a mechanic and runs his own business.

"Good," he answers. I pour him another drink, and place it in front of him. My phone vibrates so I pull it out of my pocket, glancing at the screen.

How did everything go? – Taiya

Really good. Will tell you everything when I get home. – Ryan

I put my phone away and head into the office. Time to do some work.

CHAPTER TWENTY

Taiya bounces up and down on my cock, riding me hard. I stare at her beautiful body, at the expression of ecstasy on her face and can't believe that she's mine. She's exquisite, perfect. And I've taught her just how I like it. She lowers her head to kiss me deeply, still grinding her hips, not losing rhythm. My hands squeeze the globes of her ass, lifting my hips up to meet hers. She tears her lips from mine, tilting her head back in abandon. I sit up and lean forward to capture one of her nipples in my mouth, drawing deep and sucking. It pushes her over the edge, just like I knew it would. She whispers my name as pleasure takes over her. I roll her over onto her back, still connected, and thrust into her, my mouth finding hers once more. No one has ever felt better than this, made me feel like this. Like I would do anything to protect her. Anything. Conquer the world if I had to. Taiya is the only woman I've ever made love to, and the only woman I've ever been with without using a condom. I buck into her once more as I feel myself erupt.

"You bring me to my knees," I say in a hoarse whisper as I pull out of her, resting my forehead against hers. We're both panting, and damp with sweat. Taiya doesn't say anything but kisses me sweetly, saying more with one kiss than I could ever do with words.

"I love you, wife," I say, kissing down her neck and playfully biting.

She laughs, wriggling her body. "Love you too, husband." I sigh into her hair, just enjoying the moment. "When do I get to meet your sister?" she asks after a few minutes of silence. I told her everything that happened, and how proud I am of Persephone.

"I'll invite her over for dinner or something, and everyone can meet her."

"Good," she says softly, her voice a little roughened. "Now, I want you again."

I lift my head up. "Hmmmm. Greedy little thing, aren't you?" I trail my fingers down her flat stomach. When I reach her sex, she leans into me, silently asking for more.

"When it comes to you, yes," she gasps. Good answer. I roll on top of her, pinning her with my weight.

"Thank you for coming back to me," I whisper into her ear. "Now, I'm never letting you go."

My thumb circles her clit and she gasps. I lick my tongue across the tattoo behind her ear, the one that bears my initial. My stamp of ownership.

"Keep doing that and I won't be going anywhere."

I chuckle huskily, kissing up her neck. "You never used to be this...."

"Demanding?" she says, smiling so much that her dimple pops up.

I grin. "Yes, demanding."

"I spent so long without you. I used to fantasize about what we would be doing if you were with me," she rasps.

Now that gets my interest. "What did you used to fantasize about?"

"You flew to South Africa, and surprised me. Took me to a hotel, and we made up for lost time," she says, the last line insinuating just how we made up for lost time. However my mind lingers on the first part of her comment.

I blow out a breath. "I thought about coming after you. Trust me I did, night after night. Then I kept rereading your letter." That fucking letter. "I guess I let my pride get in the way."

"It doesn't matter. We're here together now. So show me how much you love me. Maybe I'll tell you in detail exactly what happened in my mind when you found me…"

I slide into her, and show her just that.

Then she keeps her word and tells me what she used to fantasize about, and we make that a reality.

*****

The sound of someone knocking on my door wakes me up. The space next to me is empty. Taiya must have already left for work. Throwing on some shorts, I jog to the front door, wondering who the hell it could be. Opening the door I come face to face with my baby sister. I instantly go on alert, checking over her to see if she's okay.

"Sephie? Is everything okay?" I ask, ushering her into the house. I'm glad she's here, and using the address I left with her, hoping she would visit.

"Sephie? You already gave me a nick name?" she asks, raising an eyebrow and looking amused.

"Reid did actually. Now answer me, is everything all right?" I ask, frowning. We walk into the kitchen and I pour her a drink.

"Everything's fine. Can't I just drop by and see my big brother, who I only found out about the other day?" she says, sarcasm and hurt laced in her tone.

"You can come see me anytime. Hell, you can move in here if you want," I tell her, meaning every word.

She sighs, "I just got in my car and drove, and I ended up here. You gave me the address, so...."

"You're welcome here anytime," I say softly, wanting her to know that. "Now, tell me what's wrong."

"I don't want to talk about it right now. Can we just hang out?" she asks, looking around my apartment.

"Sure, I'd love that. What do you have in mind?"

Her expression turns thoughtful. "What were you going to do before I showed up?"

When I'm silent for a second, she makes a face. "Oh, crap, did I interrupt something?"

I cock my head to the side, smirking. "No, you didn't. Taiya already left for work. I was going to hit the gym to work out for a bit, then come home and shower and head to work."

She takes a huge gulp of juice. "I could use a workout." She flexes her arm. "These guns aren't as big as they used to be."

I look down at her puny arms and laugh. "Is that right?"

"Yep. Are there any hotties at your gym?" she asks, pushing her blonde hair out of her face.

"Doesn't matter, does it?"

"Why not?" she asks, her forehead creasing.

"Because once they know you're my sister, they won't even look in your direction," I say, grinning at her scowl.

"Is Reid this much of a cock block?" she asks, as if considering spending the day with Reid instead of me. I laugh so hard I have to lean on the table to hold me up. "I'll take that as a yes."

"Reid will probably just punch whoever looks at you. I'm the easy going one," I add, laughing again when her comment replays in my mind.

"Hmmmph. How about we start with food. Food is good."

I pause. "Depends what kind of food you're talking about."

She snickers. "A giant burger and fries?"

I narrow my eyes. "I knew you weren't a vegetarian!"

Now it's her turn to laugh. "You should have seen your face!"

Seeing her laugh makes me happy. I'll eat plain lettuce everyday if she laughs like that.

"You're a little shit, you know that?" I tell her, smiling.

"You have no idea, bro. But you will find out. Now, go get dressed and take a shower. You smell like sex."

I clear my throat at her comment, and then get my ass in the shower.

*****

She spins around, doing some fancy thing with her leg. She looks amazing, especially in that tight fitting thing she's wearing. I don't know how we ended up at the dance studio, but after spending the day together, Sephie wanted to meet Taiya. So here we are, watching her dance and teach a class. I discreetly adjust myself, hoping no one saw, and thinking how fucking inappropriate it is to get a hard on for my wife, while she's teaching an entire group of people.

Sephie laughs, letting me know she knows what's going on. Taiya lifts her head up at the sound, her attention now on us. She smiles as she sees me, and then looks towards Sephie and beams. I know she's been so excited to meet her new sister-in-law, and now she gets the chance.

"I'll see you all next week!" Taiya tells her class, saying her byes and walking over to us.

"Hi," she says, her eyes bright with excitement. She gives me a peck on the lips and then turns her head to my sister. "Hello Persephone, nice to meet you."

Sephie smiles. "Call me Sephie," she says, throwing me an amused smirk.

"How did you know it was my sister?" I ask, putting my arm around her.

"Because you wouldn't be stupid enough to bring any other woman here," she says, the little spitfire. "Plus you both have the exact same shade of hair. And even though her eyes are brown, they are the same shape as yours."

Sephie laughs, and makes a whipping sound. "Great, now my little sis thinks I'm whipped," I mutter, trying to hide my grin.

"Then she's smart," Taiya says. "What did you two get up to today?"

"Ryan took me on my first bike ride. Then we were going to go to the gym, but we went and ate instead," Sephie tells Taiya. "Then we went and saw a movie."

"Sounds like you two had a good time," Taiya says, smiling.

"We did," Sephie says, smiling up at me. It's the weirdest feeling, almost like we've known each other for years.

"I'll meet you guys at home then?" she asks, looking between Sephie and me.

"Yeah, and Taiya?"

She looks up at me, those beautiful green eyes wide and unguarded. "Yeah?"

I lean towards her and whisper into her ear. "You looked fucking beautiful teaching that class."

CHAPTER
TWENTY
ONE

Taiya

"Xander looks like he would be kinky in bed," Sephie says out of nowhere, causing Summer to choke on her drink.

"Why would you say that?" I ask, trying to hold in my laughter.

Sephie looks over at Xander and sighs, "I don't know just look at him. Tattoos, muscles, long hair… that intense look on his face." I look at Xander, who is sitting with Dash and Tag, and laugh. He does look like he might be intense in bed. He's currently talking with the guys, his hazel eyes sharp and intelligent.

"What do you think he's into?" I ask, actually curious now.

Sephie purses her lips in thought. "I don't know. Bondage? That would be hot."

I look at Xander once more, with raised eyebrows, speculating.

"Maybe he likes to have sex with a goat mask on, or something," Sephie jokes.

I burst out laughing, causing all the men to look over at me. Ryan walks over, like I knew he would, to see what's going on.

"What's so funny?" he asks, touching my cheek with his fingers.

"Nothing," we all say at the same time, except for Sephie who says, "Just wondering what Xander's like in bed." The woman has no filter whatsoever.

"That's my brother!" Summer whisper-yells. "Do you want to talk about how Reid is in bed?"

Sephie makes a face. "Let's make a deal to never mention this again."

"Done," Summer says, immediately.

Ryan leans down. "You better not be wondering *anything*."

I lift my chin up. "He's pretty good looking."

Ryan practically growls. "No looking."

"No looking? Can I touch then?" I taunt, flashing him an innocent look.

"You're too much," he says, grabbing my chin with his thumb and index finger and giving me a deep kiss, one completely inappropriate for public view. When he pulls back, I'm panting.

"Get a room!" Reid calls out, smirking.

"You're ruining girls' night!" Sephie huffs, gulping down her drink. Sephie, Summer and I decided to have a night out, just us girls. Isis couldn't make it, because she had to study for her exams. An hour into our evening Ryan, Reid, Xander, Dash and Tag show up, sitting at their own table, and proclaiming their own night out. We all know they just wanted to keep an eye on us. Ryan gives me another quick kiss and then re-joins his table. An hour later and the pretence is over, because we're all sitting together drinking, laughing and enjoying our time together. When I see Xander sit down next to Sephie, causally putting his arm around her, I quickly look to the twins, who are both staring at Xander's arm with narrowed eyes. Well, that's a disaster waiting to happen.

Summer and I head to the bathroom together, because apparently, even slightly tipsy girls can't go alone. I fiddle with my hair, pushing it away from my face, trying to control the wispy curls.

"I've never seen Ryan like this, you know," Summer says, retouching her clear lip gloss.

I give up on my hair and turn to face her. "What? With one woman for more than a night?"

She puts her gloss in her small clutch bag and studies me. "He was trying to get over you. Not that it worked, but he sure as hell tried."

"You can say that again," I mumble. "I know he loves me. He's really shown me how much. It's just hard to swallow the other women, you know? I know I wasn't here, blah blah, but it doesn't change how I feel."

Summer bobs her head. "Trust me, I know the feeling. Just tell yourself that you have him now and forever. All they have is a memory."

I smile dreamily. "I like that."

We walk out of the bathroom arm in arm, the smile on my face dropping as I see a woman standing next to Ryan. She puts her hand on him, saying something to him. He shakes his head at her, smiling slightly. Reid says something to him and he turns his head to look at me.

"Fuck," I see him mouth, and then it hits me why. Our deal. Looks like Ryan's not getting off tonight. I smile evilly, walking over to him and sitting down in his lap. The woman wanders away, and Ryan holds me in his arms.

"You were joking about continuing that deal, right?" he whispers into my ear. Goosebumps appear on my arms, and a shiver runs down my spine.

"Nope, not even a little bit," I say, straightening my spine.

"We'll see," he says with confidence. I know he thinks he can seduce me, but I'm not giving in this time. "You'll want me inside of you tonight."

My answer is a non-committal noise. Ryan starts rubbing his hands up my thigh, not indecently, but enough to get my motors running. He's already trying to sway my mind, sneaky bastard. Sephie's laugh causes me to look up at her, watching her facial expressions as she talks with Xander. Interesting, very interesting. Dash has stayed mostly quiet all night, nursing his drink. I don't know what's going on with him, but I hope he's okay.

"You smell so fucking good," Ryan rasps, kissing the tattoo behind my ear. It's the initial R in the middle of an infinity sign, and a symbol of my commitment to him. "And you are the most beautiful woman in this room."

I grin. "Laying it on a little thick, aren't you?"

"Yeah, well, you're not letting me go home tonight…"

My forehead creases. "What are you talking about?"

"Inside you, that's where I'm meant to be. My favourite place, and you're trying to bar me."

I blink. Then I start laughing so hard my whole body shakes. I slap at his knee. "How did you even get laid at all with those lines?"

When his eyes shutter, I see that I've actually hurt him. Shit. I kiss up his jaw then whisper into his ear, "I love you so much." I press my breasts against him, men like that, right? I cup his face and kiss him softly on his lips. I love his lips. They are fucking talented, soft and full.

"Great, now I have to watch both my brothers making out," Sephie grumbles. She looks to Xander. "Want to leave?"

That gets Ryan's attention because he turns from me to scowl at his sister. Reid stands up, and motions Xander to join him outside. Well, shit. Ryan shifts to move and I try to distract him with a wet, hard kiss. It works for a few moments but he pulls away, giving me a look that says, 'I know exactly what you're trying to do.' He stands with me in his arms, and then gently deposits me onto the chair, then goes out to follow Reid and Xander. Summer moves closer to me, eyes wide, while Sephie looks bored, and a little pissed off.

"He'll be fine," Dash says. "Xander's safe because Ryan and Reid won't touch him because of Summer. They won't want her upset."

"They can still warn him away," Summer adds.

"They can try," Sephie says, putting her drink down on the table. "Xander's pretty badass, come on."

Summer and I share a look. Xander is badass, and anyone would be stupid to mess with him, but Reid and Ryan are both trained fighters. I wonder if anyone mentioned that to their sister. About fifteen minutes pass before they all return. I check them all over for any signs of a fight, but there is nothing. Good. Xander looks slightly angry, whilst Reid and Ryan wear identical scowls. Men!

"Shall we call it a night?" I ask Summer. "I think it's time for bed."

"Sounds good," she says, standing up and grabbing her bag. "Dash do you want a ride home?"

"Yep," Dash replies, downing his drink and standing. Reid and Ryan didn't drink, so they could both drive. My gaze clashes with Ryan, green on blue, and I know that I have my own battle on my hands.

Tonight—my mission is to resist my husband.

*****

My hands fist on the sheets and my head tilts back in pleasure. Ryan kept his part of the deal and then some, that's for damn sure.

"I think I'm the luckiest woman alive," I blurt out, sighing contently. "That was amazing."

"Now are you going to make me the luckiest man alive?" comes a raspy voice. Ryan leans up, wiping his mouth with his hands, leaning over me. He's still fully dressed, while I'm completely bare, yet I don't feel any vulnerability at all. If anything, I feel beautiful and powerful, because he makes me feel that way.

"You know the rules…"

"You can't be serious," he growls. He leans down and sucks one of my nipples into his mouth, and I know then that I'm going to have to give in. For my sake, not his. He pulls back and undresses himself, quicker than I've ever seen him do so. He lies on top of me, and looks up at me, a question in his eyes.

"Fine," I snap, reaching down to position him.

Ryan chuckles, making me scowl into the dim light.

"I win," he says, slamming home.

Bastard.

*****

"What happened with Xander last night?" I ask as we're having breakfast. I tried to make bacon and eggs. I say try because the bacon came out great but the eggs are a little runny, and not that tasty. Ryan eats them anyway, not once complaining. He's probably just happy to get fed.

"Nothing. We just had a little chat," he says, emphasising the word chat.

I roll my eyes. "She's a grown-ass woman."

He lifts his head to look at me. "Yes, she is, and she can make her own decisions. We haven't been there for her, her whole life. We can't exactly walk in and take over. As much as we want to," he mutters the last part.

I look down to hide my smile. "Aren't you mature?" I tease.

He takes a bite of toast and chews then swallows. "Hey, I can control myself."

I raise an eyebrow in disagreement.

"Maybe not when it comes to you," he amends, standing up and taking his plate to the sink. "Thank you for breakfast. It was good," he lies.

"Was it?" I ask dryly, forking my eggs.

He walks past me and kisses me on the head. "It was, because you made it."

"What's your plans for the day?"

"Going to the gym, and then I have a business meeting. After, I'll be at the bar."

"Business meeting?" I ask.

"Yeah, looking at my options," he says vaguely, banding an arm around my waist and giving me a kiss. "I'll see you in the evening."

"Bye," I reply, leaning in for another kiss, this one deeper. He grabs his gym bag and walks out. I tidy up his apartment—I don't know why I keep my place when I practically live here anyway. Am I keeping it as a security net? A back-up plan? I frown, wondering if some part of me is questioning whether this will work out. Am I just waiting for something to go wrong? I don't want to be like that, but I suppose I need to be realistic. At some point, I'm going to need to take that leap and move in with him. I know he is waiting for me to decide when I'm ready. He's even spoken of buying a house for us, for when we want to start a family. While I want children, I'm not exactly ready for one just yet. I know that Ryan will be an amazing father when the time comes, because I've seen him with River. He's amazing—attentive and patient.

I lock up and head to my apartment, unlocking the door and walking in. Isis is nowhere to be found; she must be at work or uni. I call up my mum and chat with her for a while, and then I clean up my apartment. I'm about to relax and watch some TV when Summer calls asking if I want to hang out with her. Sure beats sitting around here, so I agree.

"Where are we going?" I ask as we get into her car.

"Xander's house," she says, reversing the car. "I thought we could hang out there. Is that cool?"

"Yeah, who's there?" I ask, staring out the window.

"Just Xander. My dad might drop in at some point."

"No classes today?" I ask.

"No, I'm on break now. So happy because exams were stressing me out," she says, puffing out a breath.

"I can imagine."

"So Ryan said you want to own your own dance studio one day?"

I turn to look at her. "Yes, that's my dream." I've wanted to own my own studio since as long as I can remember. I've been saving most of my money, hoping that one day I can make my dream a reality.

Summer gives me a sly smile. "I haven't seen you dance yet. Clubbing doesn't count."

I laugh softly. "You can drop by any time and see me in action."

"I might take you up on that," she replies. "I love this song," she says, turning the volume up. It's some 'Gangsta' song that Reid told me drives him insane, because she plays it on repeat. Over and over again. I think it's cute. We pull into Xander's place and spend the day watching movies and eating junk food.

I learn two things.

Xander is as sweet as he is sexy. And he definitely wants Sephie.

This ought to be interesting.

CHAPTER TWENTY TWO

Ryan

I look around the vast space, happy with what I see. This is the fifth building I've seen today, and they definitely saved the best for last. This is the perfect location. I head home and have a quick shower before I head to Knox Tavern. Tag is at the bar, Jade is standing next to him talking. He's nodding at whatever she's chatting about, but he looks like his mind is elsewhere. There are about three people sitting at the bar, and I do a double take when I see one that I recognise. I've only seen a photo of him once, when I was annoying Summer and snooping through her shit. I say a quick hello to Tag and Jade, and then stand in front of him. He looks a little bit different than the photo, older and muscular. He still has the same shaggy dark hair, blue eyes and his eyebrow pierced.

"I wouldn't be here if I were you," I say, smiling to soften my words.

He bobs his head, his lip curling. "I wanted to say hello to Summer."

I lean on the bar. "Probably not a good idea."

"Are you her man?" he asks, his eyes searching mine. I have to give him credit for meeting my stare head on.

"No. I'm the nice twin," I reply, and I hear Tag chuckle behind me.

Summer's ex-boyfriend, Quinn, lifts his beer to his mouth, his eyes giving away nothing.

"Does Summer know you're here?" I ask, waving hello as a regular walks in. "Or are you surprising her?"

"Just dropped in to say hello. I was in the area."

Yeah, I bet he was. "How did you know she worked here?"

"She mentioned it once or twice." I bet Reid doesn't know they still keep in touch, if that's the case. I leave Quinn and head into the back. Tag follows me, a curious look on his face.

"Who's the pretty boy?" he asks.

"Summer's ex."

He laughs. "Reid is going to love this."

I scoff, "You have no idea."

"How did it go today?" he asks, sitting down in my chair.

I smile. "Found the perfect place."

"She's going to love it."

"I know," I brag.

Tag runs his hand over his bald head, and stands up. He heads to the door, but before he leaves, he turns around and says, "By the way some girl asked for you today."

"Who?" I ask, cocking my head to the side.

He shrugs. "Blonde."

"No idea, probably my past trying to bite me in the ass," I mutter under my breath.

*****

The lights are all out when I get home, except for the lamp in the bedroom. I rub my eyes, tired after a long day, and look to the middle of the bed, where Taiya is fast asleep on her stomach. The sheet pools just above her ass, the sexy dimples on her lower back showing where her shirt has ridden up. Her curls fan the pillow—fuck, she's beautiful, even when she's sleeping. After a long shower, I slide in next to her completely bare. I push her hair to the side, baring her delicate neck. I place a gentle kiss on her jaw, breathing in her scent.

"Ryan?" she says softly, her voice thick.

"I'm here beautiful," I whisper back, banding my arms around her waist and pulling her into me.

She sighs, "Love you."

"Love you, too," I reply, closing my eyes and falling asleep with a smile on my lips.

*****

I pull off her blindfold, and watch as her wide green eyes take in her surroundings.

"Wha—what?" she stutters, turning in a full circle.

"Do you like it?" I ask, unable to stop the smile on my face. "It's yours."

"What do you mean?" she asks, bemused.

169

"Your dance studio. Your dream," I tell her, hoping she envisions it just the way I have. Taiya has told me in detail over the years, just how she wanted her studio to be. The mirrors, the flooring, the changing rooms, everything. I can only hope that this is what she wants, that this will make her happy.

She turns to me, her eyes wide and her mouth slightly open. "You bought me my dream dance studio?"

My heart beats faster. "Yes, I mean, it needs some work, but—"

"This is mine?" she says, cutting me off, a look of awe on her face.

"Before you start with the speech about how you can't accept it, yes, it's all yours. It's in your name, to do with as you please. You're my wife and I live to see you happy, so yes. I hope you like it."

"Like it? Are you kidding me?" she asks, jumping into my arms and kissing me.

"Thank you." Kiss. "So much." Kiss "It's perfect." Kiss. "Love you."

"You're welcome," I say softly, our eyes connecting. No words are really needed, because this one look says it all. "There's nothing I wouldn't do to make you happy." I tell her honestly, not caring what I sound like, not caring how many times I tell her, or show her how I feel. Because I *know* what it's like not to have her in my life. I know firsthand that everything is better with her around. Everything tastes better, feels better. The grass sure as hell isn't greener on the other side, and I'm never going to take this woman for granted.

Ever.

"Where are we going?" she asks, her eyes still glazed in surprise and excitement.

I take her hand in mine, our fingers intertwining. "I thought we could celebrate a little."

She looks up at me, and the expression of happiness on her face makes me want to take her right now, on the floorboards of the soon-to-be studio. When she raises an eyebrow at me in challenge, I know that she's got the same thing on her mind as I do.

"Are you sure?" I rasp, already looking around for the best spot. "It's going to be hard and fast."

"Just how I like it," she purrs, already unbuttoning her jeans.

I smirk. "Someone's eager."

"And wet," she adds, taking a step back from me. "But first you have to catch me."

It looks like she wants to play. I take a step towards her, and she retreats once more. Without warning, I run after her, lift her up and pin her against a wall.

"You asked for it," I say hoarsely, pulling off her top and pulling her bra down. "So beautiful."

"Less talking, more fucking," she replies, the minx. I grin slyly, giving her exactly what she wants, and then some.

I've never been one to back down from a challenge.

CHAPTER
TWENTY
THREE

Ryan

My day started off as any Friday would. Morning sex, check. Hit the gym, check. Work, check. I hadn't seen Taiya since morning, because she went to work, then to her mum's house. I had a pretty hectic day, between Reid telling me MMA scouts are up his ass, wanting him to fight, also him dropping the bomb that our father's been trying to get in contact with us again, obviously using his limited phone calls trying to get one of us on the line. What I didn't expect was to open my apartment door and find Taiya, sitting on the couch, staring daggers at her ex-best friend.

"What the fuck is she doing here?" I ask Taiya, my heart slamming against my chest. I refuse to let anyone ruin what Taiya and I have, what we have worked for all this time to get our relationship the way it is. I finally have my wife back, and no one is going to get between us.

"We need to talk," Sarah says, standing up. She looks the same as she did the last time I saw her. Blonde hair, brown eyes, and a model's figure. I had no idea back then that she was bat-shit crazy, but one learns from their mistakes.

"What could we possibly have to talk about?" I ask, sitting down next to Taiya and taking her hand into my lap. She allows me to do it, which is a good sign.

"I'm pregnant," Sarah says, throwing a smug look at my wife.

"And good luck to the sorry bastard that knocked you up," I tell her, confused as to why she felt the need to tell me this.

"That sorry bastard would be you," she says, crossing her arms over her chest and looking triumphant. The fuck? I have never slept with her in my life, and I haven't even seen her since the time we kissed.

"You're kidding me, right?" I say slowly, wondering what her game is. She clearly doesn't want Taiya happy, or to be with me. Why? I have no fucking idea. She's probably jealous of Taiya.

"Don't act innocent. Two months ago, we slept together and now I'm having your baby!" she says. It's official-- this bitch has lost the plot. And I'm the one who is going to have to pay for it.

I turn to Taiya. "She's lying. I would never cheat on you," I tell her, my voice taking on a pleading tone.

Taiya purses her lips, and pulls her hand away from mine. I close my eyes, squeezing them shut, knowing this is the moment where I lose her. At least until I can prove my innocence.

"Get the fuck out," Taiya says. I think she's talking to me, but I look to see her saying it to Sarah.

"Didn't you hear what I just said?" Sarah says, narrowing her eyes.

Taiya scoffs. "I heard you. And you're a lying bitch. First of all, I trust my husband. Second of all, I've read too many romance novels to know that trusting the bitch of the story, is never a good idea. If you're so adamant that the baby is his, come back when he's born and we can do a DNA test. Which will prove Ryan isn't his or her father. So if you're even pregnant at all, perhaps you should go and find the real father. I understand that might take some time to go through all the names of the men you've been with, so you best get to work." With that, she stands up and storms into the bedroom. I open and close my mouth in surprise. How amazing is my woman? I block out Sarah's whining and bitching and escort her out the door, slamming it behind her, then walk into the room where Taiya is lying on the bed, her pet bird sitting on her stomach.

"You okay?" I ask her, kneeling on the bed.

She puffs out a breath. "Yeah, it just sucks. I don't know what I ever did to her."

"She's just jealous," I tell her, lifting my hand to touch her, but moving it back when the bird makes that scary hissing noise. Taiya giggles, and almost getting my finger bitten was all worth it.

"Thank you for believing in me," I say quietly. "I thought you were going to kick my ass out."

She leans her head to the side. "You're not that stupid to lose me twice."

I chuckle at her comment. "You're right about that."

She gets up and puts Leo on top of his perch.

"Are we going to have make-up sex now?" I ask. "I could really go for some."

She puts her index finger on her chin. "I don't know. Does that count as me running into one of your ex conquests?" I can tell from her voice that she's teasing me.

"No."

"How about we just snuggle?" she says, getting back on the bed and leaning into me.

I yawn. "Snuggling is good."

I don't know how to put it into words what her trust means to me. I feel like I've just won a gold medal or something. Fuck. I'm obsessed with her.

And I wouldn't have it any other way.

*****

"You're not fucking wearing that out!" I say for the second time, hoping from my look she knows I'm serious.

"You don't control what I wear," she snaps, putting a pair of big dangly earrings into her ears.

"You might as well be naked!" I say, looking down at her beige fitted dress. It clings to every curve on her body, showing every little detail. "No, it's not happening."

"Except it is," she replies, pouting her lips as she smothers them with gloss or something.

"I'm going to be a walking erection all night," I mutter.

"Well, I'll take care of that when we get home," she says flippantly. Is she even listening to me?

"Tay, every fucking guy is going to be staring at you, going home and probably…"

She raises her hand cutting me off. "It's just a dress."

"Yeah, maybe for a fucking stripper," I say without thinking. Her face instantly changes, and I know I've pissed her right off. "I didn't mean that," I try to backtrack. "Don't be mad."

"What do I know? I'm just a stripper," she sneers, stepping out of the bathroom and into her closet, where she pulls out the highest pair of fuck me heels I've ever seen. "Yes, I think these go with tonight's theme, apparently."

Me and my big fucking mouth.

I head into the kitchen and pour myself a drink, waiting for Taiya to finish getting ready. We're heading out to dinner and then to a club with Reid and Summer for Summer's birthday. I'm chewing on an ice cube as Taiya enters the room, dressed to kill and ready to go. She has Summer's gift in her hand, in a shiny pink gift bag. I stare at her dress once more, which now looks even sexier paired with the heels. I don't know where to look… cleavage, thigh, legs or just the hourglass shape of her mid-section. My hard on isn't exactly welcomed right now, considering we need to leave and she's pissed at me. Although much can be said for angry sex…

"Are we going or are you going to stand there staring all night?" she asks, tapping her heel.

I sigh and put my glass in the sink, then walk to the front door and open it for her. "Are you bringing a jacket?" I ask, unable to contain the hope in my voice.

"No," she says sweetly, walking outside. I lock up and head to Reid's, then we all get in a cab and tell the driver directions to the restaurant.

"I love this dress," Summer says, eyeing Taiya.

"You can have it," I add in, ignoring the scowls from both women. Reid turns from the front seat with an amused smirk.

"Stop being an ass, Ry," Summer says softly, her voice laced with steel. "Taiya looks freaking amazing."

"Apparently, that's the problem," Taiya adds dryly, crossing her arms over her chest. It's Summer's birthday, which I don't want to ruin so I decide to keep my mouth shut on that topic.

"Did you like the gift, Sum?" I ask her, effectively changing the subject.

She claps her hands together. "I love it!" Taiya and I got her tickets to a concert where several different R & B and rap artists are performing. It's funny because now Reid has to go and sit through it as well, and he isn't a fan. Two birds with one stone. Make Summer happy, and annoy my brother. Taiya also got her a perfume and some other girly items. Reid turns his head once more, his blue eyes narrowed on me. He calls me a 'bastard' with that one look, and I tell him 'ha ha' with mine.

"Anything to make you happy, Sum," I say, and I see his eyes and expression soften. Oh yeah, Reid will be going to that concert; he will hold a damn sign if he has to. Anything for his woman. I take Taiya's hand in mine. She silently complies, and I rub little circles on her palm with my thumb. We share a look, and then she breaks out in a smile.

Time to enjoy the night out with my favourite people in the world.

CHAPTER TWENTY FOUR

Taiya

"What are you reading?" Ryan asks, sitting down next to me on the couch.

I lower my book to peek at him. "A romance book."

His eyebrows almost hit his hairline. "Is it porn… I mean erotica?"

I roll my eyes at him. "It does have sex in it, yes."

He grins. "Want to re-enact one of the scenes?"

I bite my bottom lip, getting a little aroused at the thought.

"You liked that idea, didn't you? Hmmm," he says, leaning forward and kissing me on my mouth.

"Am I like the heroes in your books?"

I laugh. "You wish."

"You're right. I'm way better," he says, smiling lazily.

I shake my head at his huge ego. "You need to get over yourself. Besides, the hero in this book couldn't even get it up for another woman when the love of his life left him. You definitely didn't have that problem."

Silence, then, "So his woman left then he couldn't even get it up for another woman?"

"Yep."

"I'm a man, beautiful," is his reply. "Perhaps he should see a doctor if he can't get it up."

"It's romantic," I scowl at him.

"It's romantic that he can't get a boner?"

"For anyone besides her, yes."

He sighs, and pulls me onto his lap. "Is this really in the book or is this just a dig at me?"

My body starts shaking in silent laughter. "Did you really just say that?"

I flip back a few pages in the book and find the paragraph, then show it to him. He reads it quickly, frowning.

"I can't believe you thought I made it up," I mutter, closing the book.

He places a kiss on the back of my neck. "Apparently, I know nothing of romance books."

"That's okay. I love you anyway," I say, leaning back into him. "I can't remember the last time we both had a day off and just did nothing."

"I wouldn't say we are going to be doing nothing," he says, reaching his hand down to cup my breast. "I don't think I will ever get enough of you."

The man is seriously insatiable. Not that I'm complaining. I suck in a breath when he turns my body, lowers his head and gently bites down on my breast through the soft cotton of my white dress. I watch as he then moves to my mouth, giving me a kiss that makes my panties wet. I tangle my hands in his hair, pulling on the ends, silently demanding for more. I straddle his lap, grinding myself into him, letting him know I mean business.

"Insatiable girl," he mumbles, voicing my earlier thoughts about him. I grin against his mouth in reply, and resume kissing him with everything I have. My hands soon start to wander, running up his six pack of abs, feeling each sculptured curve. I end the kiss, moving my hands to pull his T-shirt off and throwing it behind me. I sink my teeth into my lip as I take him in. I don't think I'll ever get tired of seeing him. Eye-fucking candy. And he's all mine.

"Did you just mumble 'mine'?" he asks, looking a mixture between turned on and amused. His lids are heavy, but there is a slight smirk playing on his lips.

"Did I?" I ask breathlessly, my eyes roaming down his body.

"Yes, you did, and I'm pretty sure that's my line," he says, running his large hands up my thighs, reaching for the hem of my dress and lifting it up over my head. The dress gets caught in my mass of curls, so I reach up and help him get it off. "Beautiful," he breathes, running his thumb over my lace bra. I lick my lips as he swipes my nipple through the material. Impatient, I lean back and unclasp my bra, letting it fall, sliding the straps off my arms and throwing it on the floor. Ryan is sitting there in nothing but his jeans, and I'm straddling him in nothing but a pair of tiny silk leopard-print panties. I imagine we make quite the picture. I place my hands on his chest, my darker skin contrasting against his fair. I trail my hands down to undo his top button, trying to pull his jeans down with no luck.

"I need them off!" I growl. "Why do you have to wear such tight jeans?" I complain.

Ryan blesses me with a deep chuckle, lifting his hips up and helping me pull his jeans down to his thighs. I can see his cock straining through his boxers, and I grin pulling those down as well.

"There you are," I mumble, lowering my body onto the floor so I'm on my knees before him. I lick my lips and look up at him.

Then I rock his world.

*****

"Here's your drink, thank you," I tell the man, sliding over his scotch. I don't know how I ended up working at the bar tonight, when I have no idea what the hell I'm doing. Jade is sick, Tag is off today and has gone away with his little girl, and Summer and Reid are on the other side of town spending some time with Sephie. That leaves Ryan and me at the bar. And it's a disaster. I'm so lucky to have someone as patient as Ryan as my husband, considering I've only been here two hours and already have dropped a glass and made two wrong drinks. I turn to look at him, charming a group of people and making five drinks quicker than I make one. Yeah, I think I'll definitely stick to dancing.

"You okay?" Ryan mouths, and I nod and force a smile, turning to serve the next person in line. She orders a cocktail I've never heard of, so I quickly look down at the laminated chart Ryan gave me to use, showing me what to put in each drink.

An hour later, the bar has died down and I smile when I see a familiar face.

"Hello stranger," he says, and I instantly feel bad that we haven't spent any time together since Ryan and I got back together, apart from one family dinner.

"Hey Scott, how are you?" I ask, leaning across the bar to give him a peck on the cheek.

"Good, how are you? I feel like I haven't seen you in forever," he says, drumming his fingers on the bar table.

I wince. "I know. I'm sorry. What are you doing tomorrow?" Ryan is just going to have to suck it up, because I don't want to be the person that ditches her friends the minute she gets into a serious relationship. Marriage. Whatever. Scott was there for me when I was heartbroken and I'll never forget that.

"I have work all day tomorrow, but I'm free on Wednesday," he says, smiling welcomingly.

"Shame, you're busy Wednesday night, Tay," comes a smooth deep voice from behind me.

I turn and frown. "Busy doing what?" I have two dance classes and that's about it.

"Busy fucking me," he says in a serious tone. I look at him, blink twice. Open my mouth, then snap it shut. I swear I thought I just heard him say...

"Did you just say...?"

"Yes," he says, before I can finish my sentence.

I tighten my lips and narrow my eyes. "Don't be rude," I whisper-shout, then turn back to Scott, whose wide-eyes are solely on Ryan. "Sorry," I mouth, trying to smile a little to make the situation less awkward. Which it doesn't, at all. I clear my throat and then continue. "Wednesday works fine."

"You're not going out with him, Tay," Ryan says, his tone final.

I bite the inside of my cheek. "Since when do you control my life?"

"Since you're trying to spend the day alone with a man who clearly wants in your pants," he says, his eyes still on Scott, who looks like he wants to be anywhere but here right now. And I don't blame him. Even I want to be anywhere but here. I turn my back to Ryan, hoping he gets the point. Of course, being Ryan he doesn't, and decides to move in closer, getting in my personal space.

"I don't want you going somewhere alone with him," he says, his voice softer now. He must have noticed I was pissed off and is trying a different approach. Smart man.

I give Scott a drink on the house and he goes back to the table with his friends. I really don't like being spoken to like that in public. If Ryan had his concerns, he should have pulled me aside and spoken to me quietly, not pee all over me in front of anyone within earshot. I serve another three people and I feel his gaze on me the entire time, but I don't look at him. I just try and pretend he's not there, which is pretty hard. It's extremely difficult to ignore a tall, muscled, sexy man, standing there, watching your every move.

"How long are you going to give me the silent treatment?" he asks, standing directly behind me and gripping my waist gently.

I drop the tea towel in my hand and sigh. "And this is why husbands and wives shouldn't work together."

He kisses the top of my head, and turns me around to face him. "I was jealous," he admits. I lift my gaze to him, surprised by his admission.

"Jealous?" I repeat softly, wanting more of an explanation.

"I know you two are just friends, but... he knows you. He knows you well, and I don't like that. I want you to be only that close with me," he says, pursing his lips.

"He's just a friend, Ryan."

He rubs the back off his neck. "A friend who you were around while we were separated. I don't know. I'm not good at explaining things. I just don't like it. I know he has feelings for you; trust me I know. You can deny it all you want, and fuck, I don't blame him because you're amazing. But, you're mine, and I don't want him even thinking he has a chance."

"Ryan--"

"And how would you feel if I was hanging around with a female friend?" he asks, raising an eyebrow.

I puff out a breath, not liking that one bit.

"My point exactly," he says, looking smug.

I suck in my cheeks. "He doesn't want me. He knows that we're only friends. Do you really want me to be the type of person that just ditches all the people that were there for her when my heart was broken?"

"At least I fixed it," he mutters under his breath, looking down.

"I didn't say that to make you feel bad. I was just trying to get you to understand."

"I know," he says, placing his hand on my back. He's about to say something else when more customers walk up to the bar, wanting drinks. "To be continued later."

"Okay," I say, sighing and looking over at Scott who has his eyes on me, a frown marring his expression. Great, he probably thinks Ryan's controlling me and I'm some weak woman who lets him walk all over me. I stock up the fridge, and tidy everything up as much as I can. I'm collecting empty bottles from one of the tables when Scott walks up to me and pulls something off my back.

"What's that?" I ask, looking at the piece of paper in his hand. He raises an eyebrow and hands it over to me. The paper reads, 'property of Ryan' and he's stuck it onto my back with a piece of sticky tape, like one would a 'kick me' sign. I scrunch the paper up, not knowing whether to laugh or yell. I catch Ryan's gaze and he gives me a boyish grin and a wink. I shake my head at him, and throw the ball of paper, aiming for his head. He ducks, his shoulders shaking with laughter.

"I'm heading out," Scott says from next to me. I turn to him, and give him a chaste kiss on his cheek.

"Nice seeing you, Scott. I'll message you about catching up, okay?"

He smiles and nods, waving once before leaving with his friends. I pick up another empty beer bottle and walk towards the recycling bin, putting them in. Everyone in the bar starts to clear out, and I for one am grateful.

"What time do we close?" I ask him as I approach.

"In about ten minutes. Are you okay?" he asks, taking me into his arms. "You look tired."

I hide my face into his chest. "I'm fine. A little hungry."

"Better go feed my woman then… hmmm," he rumbles, squeezing me tighter. "I'll quickly close up and then we can go and get something."

"What do you want me to do?" I ask, looking around.

"The place is sparkling; you've done enough. Why don't you sit down and I'll make you a drink?" he says, lifting me in his arms. He gropes my ass a little before placing me down on the seat.

"Perve!" I tease, sticking my tongue out.

He stares at my tongue. "Don't give me any ideas."

"Like I'd need to!" Let's just say Ryan can be very… creative.

"True," he says, smirking.

"And no thanks on the drink. I'll grab something when we head out."

"You sure?"

"Yeah, I'm not really thirsty. I'm sure I will be later though," I say, my tone making an innocent sentence sound extremely dirty.

His lips curve into a panty-dropping smile, and I watch as he goes about his business, closing up and emptying the cash register. About fifteen minutes passes before he walks back over and lifts me off the stool.

"Let's go feed my girl."

CHAPTER TWENTY FIVE

Taiya

The next morning, I don't know why the fuck Sarah is standing by my car, but it's taking everything in me to not jump into my car and run her over. I don't know what went wrong along the way with our friendship, but as far as I'm concerned, she can go to hell. I know I'm a good person. I've never screwed anyone over or betrayed anyone. I'm as loyal as they come, and I deserve a friend that is more than a trifling whore with a thing for my husband.

"What do you want?" I snap, looking for my keys in my oversized handbag.

She purses her lips. "Can't an old friend say hello?"

I laugh without humour. "Cut the shit. What do you want? To convince me Ryan slept with you? Because we all know that's bullshit."

"You don't know shit, Taiya," Sarah says angrily, her cheeks going red.

"I know that you can go get fucked," I tell her, finally finding my keys, pulling them out and pressing the button to open the car door.

"Fine, we never slept together. I'll admit it. I lied. But I kissed Ryan more than once. Maybe you should ask him about that?" she sneers, a look of hate appearing on her face.

"What the fuck did I ever do to you?"

She shrugs. "Everything came so easy to you. You deserved to be taken down a notch."

"It's not high school anymore, Sarah. Grow the fuck up and move on with your life." With that, I get into my car and drive off.

Her words run through my mind on the way home. Could she have been telling the truth? Ryan told me he hadn't seen her again. However, I suppose I'd be stupid to blindly believe everything a man tells me. I push Sarah out of my mind and turn up the volume on the radio. John Legend's 'All of Me' plays and I sing along with the music. I drive to the supermarket to pick up a few things for the house, and then head straight home. Ryan said we can start fixing up the studio next week, and I can't wait. I still can't believe he did this for me, such a huge gesture. It's like all of a sudden, everything is going perfectly in my life and I'm not going to let anyone walk in and ruin it for me. Ryan and I deserve our happily ever after.

*****

I can tell something has upset Xander by the way he's brooding, but I don't know if it's my place or not to ask him. I'm at the bar, waiting for Ryan to finish work. I turn and watch Xander, who is sitting all alone at the farthest table. After he slams his phone down on the table, I slide into the seat opposite him.

"Is everything okay?" I ask softly, my gaze dropping to the tattoos covering his neck. His whole neck is now pretty much covered. I never thought I would have found that attractive, but on him, it looks hot. He also seems a lot older than his age. I know he's a few years younger than me. He's definitely an old soul; I can tell that by looking into his eyes. Xander is an enigma, that's for sure. Something tells me there is more to him than his tough exterior.

He sucks in his lips and eyes me warily. "Not really."

Okaaaaay then. "If you want to talk, I'm a good listener."

Silence. He picks up his beer and takes a sip, tilting his head back. The silence gets a little awkward, and I'm just about to stand and leave when he finally speaks.

"I like Sephie," is all he says, looking down at the table.

I frown. "So that's a good thing, right?"

He pauses, then leans back in his chair. "It was."

"And now it isn't?" I ask, trying to read between the lines of his vague comment.

He stares at me with his hazel eyes, and I shift in my seat, a little unnerved by being pinned by his steady gaze. "Ryan's a lucky man, you know."

My eyes widen. That's not what I expected him to say at all. "Thank you."

His lip twitches, before he slowly nods his head. "Summer really likes you."

I smile. "I really like her too. By the way, don't think I didn't notice the subject change."

Xander chuckles, and it's a deep husky sound. "I know. Bottom line is Seph and I aren't going to work out."

"Why?" I ask nosily, probably overstepping my bounds. I can't help but be curious. They only met recently, so I don't know what it could be that already has them pulling away.

His gaze darkens, and I instantly regret asking, not that he answers me anyway. Instead, Ryan, who walks up to the table and tells me we can leave if I'm ready, saves him. I stand up, stop at Xander, lean down and give him a kiss on the cheek. Then I take Ryan's hand and leave to go home.

*****

"Who are you again?" Isis asks me, standing at the door with her arms crossed.

I wince. "I know I haven't been here and I'm sorry. I'm the worst roomie ever. I know."

"Why don't you just move in with him? I won't be upset. You're hardly here anyway. Oh, hey, maybe Sephie will move in," Isis says.

I sigh. "I know. I think that's probably a good idea."

"We can still see each other. It's still in the same building," she says, obviously noting my sad expression.

I nod twice. "Yeah, you're right." I walk into the living room and flop down onto the couch. "How's everything anyway?"

She sits down next to me. "Work, uni, you know how it goes. All work and no play."

I raise an eyebrow at her.

"Okay, well, some play." We both burst out laughing.

"Tag?"

She pouts. "Uninterested apparently."

I change the subject. "You want to go out for dinner tonight? Just us?" I ask her. I miss Isis, and I feel bad that I haven't spent much time with her.

Her pale eyes light up. "Sounds good. And I know just the place. We should see a movie too."

"Sounds good. I'm going to go start packing up my room," I tell her, standing up and walking to my room. I open the door and stare at all my stuff. No time like the present. I start pulling out my clothes, imagining the look on Ryan's face when I tell him I'm officially moving in.

CHAPTER TWENTY SIX

Ryan

Taiya tells me to come to her apartment. The door is unlocked, causing me to frown at the thought of anyone who could just walk in. I call out Taiya's name, walking into her room to find her standing there, smiling at me.

"Hey beautiful," I say, looking around her room in confusion. It is empty. "What's going on?" I ask her, my brows scrunching. Is she moving?

"Surprise," she says, closing the space between us and throwing her arms over my shoulders. "I'm all yours."

My eyes widen as I realise what she's telling me. "You're moving in with me? Officially?"

"Yep," she says, making me the happiest man on the planet. She starts kissing me and making little moaning noises that go straight to my cock. I look around, finding no surface I can make love to her on besides the floor and the wall. She jumps up and wraps her legs around me, pushing her body against mine.

The wall it is.

We make love for the last time ever in her apartment.

*****

I don't think words can express my happiness that Taiya finally moved in. I grin to myself, as I get on my bike to go for a ride. I haven't done this in ages, ride just for the sake of it, to enjoy the freedom. Two hours later, I end up at the gym. I see Reid standing there, looking a mixture of bored and agitated, an older man standing next to him talking animatedly. I quickly head to the change room and remove my shoes, jeans and T-shirt, sliding on some sweats instead and leaving my chest bare. When I walk back towards the octagon, Reid spots me but his expression doesn't change.

"What's going on?" I ask him as I approach.

The other man, who looks to be in his forties but in good shape, replies, "He's a good fighter."

My eyes flit back to Reid. "I know he is. Who are you?"

"MMA scout," Reid replies, not looking happy about it.

The scout takes a step closer. "I have an eye for talent. Trust me, you could be the best."

"I don't fight anymore," Reid replies, stepping away from the man and walking to pick up his water bottle.

"Yeah and what a fucking waste," the scout mutters under his breath.

"I don't think that's any of your business," I snap, losing my composure. "If my brother wants to contact you, he will."

"If you don't fight anymore, what are you doing here? Still practising every day. Don't you dare try and tell me you don't love it, because the proof is right here," he calls out to Reid, his arms motioning around the gym. With that, walks off and exits the gym. Reid shrugs his shoulders in a 'what the fuck can you do' kind of way. I shake my head at him, and start shaking my limbs and bouncing on my toes, needing to warm up. I want to ask Reid what's going on in that head of his, but I don't for two reasons. One, he will talk to me when he wants to, and two, if he says he wants to fight and Summer tries to ask me about it... yeah I'd rather stay out of that.

"Come on, bro, I'll go easy on you," I say, trying to lighten up his mood.

He gives me a crooked smile, so like my own. "Let's see what you got."

*****

"That's everything unpacked," I say, unable to contain my smile. I pick up the last few boxes and put them in a stack in the corner of the living room. "There's no escaping now."

Taiya laughs, taking her mug and putting it into the sink. "It feels right."

"I'm glad you think so," I say, walking up and taking her in my arms. "Do you want to go out for dinner?"

199

"Yeah, then maybe we could go and see how Isis is handling her first shift at the bar," she says. Isis wanted a job, and I could always use some extra help. I don't really need to work as much as I do, but I like being productive and keeping busy. It's basically family and friends that work there, so we end up laughing as much as we do work.

"Okay."

"Did you ever think we would be like this again?" she asks, her stunning green eyes looking up at me. I feel a pang in my chest, like I do every time she looks at me.

"Together?"

She nods. "Yeah. Back together, stronger than ever."

I pull her into me. "I dreamed about it, but I wasn't sure it would ever happen." And that thought was what drove me into casual sex. I wanted the connection, but knew there was never going to be anyone that I'd love as much as I love Taiya. I realise now what an idiot I was. I should have fought harder instead of feeling sorry for myself and letting my pride get in the way. However, if I had to go through all of that again to be here now, in this moment, then I'd do it.

She sighs softly, burying her face into my chest, almost like she would crawl inside me if she could. She grips her fingers into the material of my T-shirt, pulling down a little. "We have dinner with my mum tomorrow."

"Sounds good." I love Rita. She's a great woman and raised two amazing girls. "Have you spoken to Claire recently?" I ask, referring to Taiya's sister.

"Yeah, we had a video chat the other day. She said she will try and come to visit us at the end of the year." Claire moved overseas just after Taiya and I got married. "I hope she does."

"Maybe we could go and see her if she can't make it?" I say.

She lifts her head from my chest to look me in the eye. "Really?"

"Sure. Reid's here to manage the bar, so why not. We could go anywhere you wanted to go." I want to take her everywhere, spoil the shit out of her. I've always wanted to take her to the Maldive Islands, which I know is where she wanted to go on our honeymoon, but we couldn't afford it back then. Now, I can give her everything she deserves and more.

Taiya Rose Knox will never want for anything.

*****

I watch as Isis serves a group of guys, making sure they don't overstep any boundaries or try anything. Her first shift seems to be going well, and she has Tag and Jade showing her the ropes. Taiya sits on my lap and takes a sip of my bottle of water. I kiss her on her delicate neck, making her giggle as she puts the bottle back on the table.

"Did you enjoy your dinner?" I ask her.

She raises her eyebrow. "I practically inhaled yours and mine."

I hide my grin into her neck, not bothering to try and deny it. I love the fact that Taiya doesn't try and starve herself, rather she eats healthily, and now and again lets herself indulge. I don't mind what size she is, but I know that as a dancer, she needs to be fit and strong, even though she doesn't dance professionally.

"Did you ask Sephie if she wanted to move into the apartment with Isis?" she asks, frowning. I know that she worries about Isis being able to pay the rent without her living there to share the bills.

"I rang her but she didn't answer. I'll try again tomorrow," I tell her, pulling her up on my lap. I hope my sister does move in, then she will be closer so I can keep an eye on her. And see her more often, of course.

"Okay, I hope she says yes."

"Me too. You want to head home?" I ask her, getting a little excited with her sitting on my lap.

"Yeah, I'll just go and say bye to Isis," she says, getting up and walking to the bar. I'm not going to deny it, my eyes are glued to her ass the entire time.

"Hi," purrs a vaguely familiar voice, interrupting my view of the greatest ass of all time.

I look up into the face of someone I'd prefer to never see again. "What are you doing here, Sarah?"

She puts on a fake sad face. Fuck, how was Taiya ever friends with this girl? "I wanted to apologise to Taiya."

"Why bother? She isn't going to be friends with you again, you should just leave her alone," I say, standing up and turning my head to look for Taiya. I see her standing in front of the bar, leaning over it to talk to Isis.

"Scared that I'm here, are you?" she asks, pushing her chest out. "Or maybe it's Taiya that feels threatened about you being in my company?"

"Why would I be? We only kissed, and Taiya knows about it. I'm a little more nervous about her," I say pointing to a woman that I'd slept with before. She waves at me and I cringe, but give a slight wave back. Sarah apparently takes offence to something I said, because an evil sneer appears on her what could be pretty face.

"What the fuck are you doing here?" Taiya says, as she walks up and stands at my side. "Are you stalking me now?"

Wait, what?

"You wish. I just wanted to talk to you for a second," Sarah says, an almost vulnerable look flashing on her face before she masks it. I think Taiya notices it too, because she tilts her head slightly and says, "You have five minutes."

I'm about to object when Taiya bends and gives me a possessive kiss. "Five minutes," she repeats, "I'll just be out the front."

Not liking the idea of my woman standing outside, I shake my head no. "Use my office." Taiya nods and heads to the office, Sarah following behind her. What the fuck is going on here? This is like, the kiss that never ends. A kiss! Okay, maybe she took her top off too, but fuck. I don't know why she is still in our lives and I wish that she would just leave us alone. Instead of sitting around and doing nothing, I decide to help out at the bar until they are done.

And then I want to know what the hell Sarah would possibly have to talk to Taiya about.

CHAPTER TWENTY SEVEN

Taiya

After Sarah enters, I close the door behind us. I stand in front of the door facing her, my arms crossed against my chest. "What?" I ask rudely, wanting to get this conversation over with.

She looks down at her feet, as if gathering her thoughts. "I kissed Ryan for a reason."

I scoff. "Yeah to try and seduce him."

"No, well, yes," she says, cringing. "I wanted him. The way he treated you... I wanted that."

I wait for her to continue.

"You know that my dad died..."

I nod. "Yes, I used to know everything about you. We *were* best friends after all." I don't even want to think about all the things we'd been through together, all our good memories. And there were some good memories. Also the bad memories, like when her dad died, I was there for her as best as I could be at that age. I know her mum and her didn't always see eye to eye, and she took the death of her dad really hard.

"Shit was going on at home with my mum. I was jealous, okay? You had everything I wanted, including Ryan, so I went for it. I'm sorry."

"Okay," I say, dragging out the word. What does she want from me? Her being sorry doesn't change anything; she still betrayed me, and she still was a shit friend.

I move away from the door, hoping she takes the hint and leaves. "You know if you had problems in your life, I would have been there for you no matter what."

"I know. And I didn't mean what I said about Ryan. There was no second kiss. I'm sorry."

With that, she walks out of the door, and hopefully out of my life.

*****

I told Ryan about Sarah's apology. I know he felt like shit, because he was involved too, and we were trying to move on from everything that happened. There is no room for lies or omissions in marriage, so even though it hurt to bring everything up again, I told him what she said and we spoke about it. Ryan went quiet for a few moments, then said he was sorry for everything, including being a part of me losing my best friend, then said he's going to talk with Reid. He gave me a simple kiss, then left the apartment. I cleaned up the kitchen, trying to keep myself busy. When two am arrived and he still wasn't home, I sent Summer a text message. She replied instantly and said Reid and Ryan were talking and playing with Reid's PS4. I take a warm bath, sipping on a glass of red wine, trying not to get my favourite paperback wet.

When the water turns cold, I get out and dry myself, then slip on my leopard-print robe. I'm about to head to bed when I hear Ryan coming home.

"Hey," I say as he walks into our bedroom.

"Hey, sorry I was gone so long," he says, sitting on the bed and taking off his shoes.

"Don't worry about it," I say. I've been around them enough to know that there are certain times they just need to be in each other's company. I would never hold that against him.

I walk over to him and sit down next to him on the bed. I lay my head on his shoulder, wanting to be close to him, to touch him any way I can. "I'll have a shower, give me a sec," he says, kissing me on the forehead and then heading to our bathroom. I slide to the middle of the bed and get under the covers. I hear the shower turn on, and I close my eyes for a second.

*****

I grab my phone to check the time, six am. What am I doing up so early? I turn to face Ryan, who is fast asleep on his back, his blond hair partially covering one of his eyes. It should be illegal to be that gorgeous first thing in the morning. Deciding to wake him up in a way I know he will appreciate, I scoot down the bed, lifting the covers over my head. Kneeling, I bend low and find Ryan's naked hip, placing soft kisses on it. I nibble down his thigh, grinning when I hear a moan escape his mouth. I take him into my hand and slide him into my mouth. I know he's awake when I hear him utter a curse, followed by the blanket disappearing. His hand reaches down to push the hair out of my face.

"Fuck, I love you," he says hoarsely, his voice husky and low. My mouth tugs into another grin, then I lick my lips and get to work.

CHAPTER TWENTY EIGHT

Ryan

"Where have you been recently? You've been missing in action," I ask Sephie. She finally rang me back, and I asked if she wanted to come over for lunch.

She gives me an odd look before answering. "Just busy with work and stuff."

"Okay, let me know if you need anything."

"I'm not going to take your money, Ryan," she says, puffing out a breath that makes her hair blow off her face.

"Trust me, I know. But we're more than happy to help you with whatever you need."

"I know. I know. I just like to do things for myself. I don't like handouts," she says, looking down at her jean-clad knees.

"It's not a handout, Seph. What's mine is yours and the same goes with Reid, so don't even think like that. You're not a burden. We love having you in our lives," I tell her, hoping she understands it's the truth.

She nods. "I know. You've never made me feel like I was a burden."

"Good."

"So what's for lunch? I'm assuming Taiya didn't cook." We both laugh.

"No, she definitely didn't. I ordered pizza. Hope that's okay?"

"Sounds good to me. So have you spoken to Xander recently?" she asks, not looking me in the eye as she says his name.

I still. "I've seen him a few times, why?"

She clears her throat. "Oh, no reason."

She's hiding something. What the hell happened between Xander and her? "Is everything all right then?"

She rolls her eyes. "Everything's fine. So when are you and Taiya going to have kids?" she asks, effectively changing the subject. She's a smart one my sister. For most men, that question would render them speechless and they would lose their train of thought. Not me though.

"As soon as Taiya is ready. I'd have one right now if she wanted to," I say, smiling at her cheekily.

Her eyes widen. "Okay, I wasn't expecting that answer."

"I know," I reply. "Now what's really going on?"

She opens her mouth to talk when the bell rings. Saved by the pizza.

"Hold that thought, Seph," I say, grabbing my wallet and walking to the door. I pay the deliveryman, giving him a hefty sized tip, and close the door with a push of my hip. I walk into the lounge room and put the two pizzas on the coffee table.

"Do you want something to drink?" I ask her.

"I'll grab it," she says, walking into the kitchen. She comes out with two bottles of water, and hands one over to me.

"Thanks." I watch her for a few seconds, trying to figure out what's going on with her. She has an almost guilty vibe going on. I decide not to push her. I guess she will talk about whatever is going on when she's good and ready.

"Do you want to watch *Animal Planet*?" she asks, smiling like she already knows the answer.

I put the TV on, and grab a slice of pizza.

*****

Taiya walks into the apartment straight from work. She's wearing those tight stretchy black pants I love so much, and a tight black top. Her bag is across the shoulder; her hair up in what I call her 'dancer's bun' even though her curls are currently trying to escape it.

"Did you stay home all day?" she asks, throwing her bag on the floor and coming forward to greet me.

"I did. Seph came over, and then Reid came over. We hung out." She jumps into my lap and kisses me. "How was your day?"

"It was good. I'm teaching the little kids a new routine," she says, running her fingers through my hair.

"How old are they?"

"Between seven and twelve."

"You know you are going to have to quit that place to work on your studio."

She sighs. "Yeah, I know."

"And you can finally use that credit card I got you." A credit card in Taiya's name arrived in the mail a few weeks back. She wasn't happy about it, but too bad.

She makes a noncommittal noise.

"And I have a surprise for you."

She instantly perks up. "A surprise?"

"Yeah, well. I was wondering if you wanted to renew our wedding vows. I've got everything planned and I thought—" She cuts me off with a kiss.

"I'd love to renew our vows," she says, brightening with happiness.

"Good," I say softly, cupping her face with my hands. "Make me the happiest man in the world, for the second time."

"Better be the last time," she mock growls, and I bite gently on her lower lip.

"Damn straight it will be the last time. Except maybe when we're old and you want to renew our vows again. We'll still be that in love in our old age."

"That confident, are you?"

"You're a sure thing, baby." She pinches me, making me laugh. "I'm going to make sure we stay strong. Don't you worry."

Her face goes soft.

"You aren't going to swoon are you?" I tease, kissing her on her nose.

"I love you, Ryan," she whispers.

"I love you too, beautiful."
More than life itself.

CHAPTER TWENTY NINE

Ryan

"Since you're renewing your vows, do we get to throw you a bachelor party? You didn't have one last time," Reid says, rubbing his hands together, reminding me of Mr. Burns from the *Simpsons*.

"If I get a buck's night, that means Taiya gets a hen's night," I cringe at the idea of some stripper waving his penis around my woman's face.

Reid laughs. "You should see your face. Live a little, baby brother."

"Is Summer going to have a hen's party?" I ask, looking at him expectantly.

He shrugs. "She will probably want one. It's a rite of passage."

I sigh, scrubbing my hand over my face. "I'll talk to Taiya and see what she thinks."

"All right. Ask her for your balls back while you're at it."

"Coming from you, that's hilarious."

"I need to start planning. This buck's night is going to be insane," he says, mostly to himself.

"I haven't said yes."

"You haven't said no either."

We give each other identical shit-eating grins.

"I think it's a good idea," Taiya says, as she walks into the room with Summer by her side. They spent the day at the spa, having a girls' day. "What do you think, Summer? Think you can organise something wild?"

"Hell, yeah I can," Summer replies, her brown eyes twinkling. I can just imagine what she's going to plan.

I grit my teeth, throwing Reid a 'see what I told you asshole' look. Reid smiles, not looking apologetic in the least. "I don't know…" I start, looking back at Taiya. I rub the back of my neck. I don't exactly relish the idea of her going 'wild.'

"It will be fun," Taiya says, walking towards me, sitting down and wrapping her arms around me. I bury my face in her hair, her scent making me dizzy.

"Okay," I say, finding myself unable to say no to her. "How about we separate for an hour or two then meet up and all go out together to celebrate."

Reid starts laughing, like I said something hilarious. Taiya agrees, saying that that's a good idea. Crisis averted. Nothing like a good old compromise.

"I can't remember the last time I went to a strip club," Reid says, leaning back in his chair. "Oh, now I remember. It was that time…" he trails off when he sees the look on Summer's face.

"It was that time what?" Summer asks him in a fake sweet tone.

Reid clears his throat. "It was before you."

"I'd hope so," she says instantly, her voice as dry as it can get. "Well, at least now you have an excuse to go to one."

"Don't worry, Summer. I'm sure you can find us a good male strip club," Taiya says, adding in her two cents. More like her not wanting to see Summer get upset.

Summer smiles and nods. "This is true. When are we doing this?"

"How about next weekend?" Taiya says. I don't like the fact she's obviously excited about this.

"Sounds good. When are you two renewing your vows?"

"Next month," I tell Summer. And I can't fucking wait. Taiya runs her hand on my thigh, applying pressure gently. She can't wait too.

"Shall we get going?" Reid asks, standing up. We're all going to Jack's house for dinner. I'm looking forward to seeing River. Mia said we could pick him up on the way. Taiya's mum will be there too, and it's the first time we will all be together. I'm really looking forward to it. The girls go do whatever they have to do, and then we go to spend the evening with our extended family.

*****

"You're wearing that? To a male strip club?" I ask, my mouth practically hanging open. The week passed with a blur, and sooner than I knew it, the night of the hen's/buck's was upon us. I don't know where Taiya, Summer, Isis and Jade are going, and they don't know where Reid, Xander, Dash, Tag and I are going. Hell, I don't even know where we're going. Only Reid does, and the rest of us are being surprised. I'm wearing my usual jeans and a black shirt, but Taiya has decided to go all out. The girls have apparently decided to dress up tonight, with a shared theme. Schoolgirls. My wife is dressed up like a slutty schoolgirl in a white shirt, tied around her waist, the top buttons undone to show off her red lacy bra. She is wearing a thin black tie around her neck, a red tartan looking mini skirt, white knee high socks and black high heels. Her normally unruly curls have been straightened and are worn in two pigtails. I adjust myself and scowl at her. I think my jeans just got about two sizes too tight.

"Yeah, I'm wearing this. I think it's cute, and we're all going to be dressed like this," she says, adding more bright red lipstick. Unable to take my eyes off her, I stare at the few inches of her bare stomach, and then move lower to the short skirt, hugging her round shapely behind. Fuck me.

"I don't like this," I breathe, rubbing my hands over my mouth. "Not one fucking bit."

Taiya frowns. "Don't ruin my night, Ryan."

Fuck. Fuck. Fuck. "Okay, you're right. But if you have any trouble, please call me immediately, and keep that outfit on because I'm fucking you with it on at the end of the night."

Her eyes widen at my demand. "Yes, Mr. Knox," she replies in a sweet tone which goes straight to my cock.

"You better be wearing panties with that skirt."

She grins and lifts up her skirt, showing me barely there red lace. Great, just fucking great. I'm contemplating cancelling this whole night when the doorbell rings. I stare at my wife longingly for a second before I go and answer the door.

"Why do you look like someone ran over your puppy? It's your fucking buck's night!" Reid says, walking in carrying two bottles of alcohol. Summer walks in behind him, dressed in the same sort of outfit as Taiya, but a less slutty version.

"Hey Ry," she says, kissing me on the cheek.

"Hey Sum, you look pretty," I tell her. I turn to see Taiya standing there, giving me a strange look. She couldn't be mad about Summer, could she? Summer is like family to me. She has no need to be jealous. I remind myself to have a talk with her about it when we're alone. Taiya and Summer start chatting and Reid pours me a drink. About an hour later, the girls' limo pulls up, and Summer and Taiya head out. They are picking up the rest of the girls on the way, except for Sephie because she said she had to work.

Reid and I walk the girls out, and I open the door for them, but pull Taiya aside just as she's about to get into the limo.

"Are you okay?" I ask her, my eyes searching hers.

She nods. "Yeah, I'll see you later tonight."

I lower my head to give her a possessive kiss, reminding her who she belongs to.

"Message received," she mumbles before she gets in.

I elbow Reid who is making out with Summer, but he ignores me and keeps kissing her. She finally pulls away, and she slides in after Taiya. I close the door, and watch as the limo drives away.

"Let the fun begin!" Reid says, ringing up a taxi to come get us. I sigh, and stare at the limo until it's out of sight.

*****

"You sure you don't want another drink?" Tag asks me as we leave the second bar. Bar hopping. I can't remember the last time I did this. We closed Knox Tavern for the night, because everyone was going out. I really need to hire at least one new employee that isn't one of my good friends. I stare at Reid who is grinning at something Dash said, and Xander who has been suspiciously quiet all night.

"No, I'm good. Where are we going next?" I ask Tag.

He shrugs, and asks, "Reid, where we going?"

"Strip club," Reid replies, turning to look at us.

"What strip club are we going to?" Xander asks, his lips tightening.

"Wait and see," Reid says. We all get into another Taxi, and drive for about fifteen minutes until we reach our destination. Reid pays the taxi driver, and we all get out and stare at the building. We walk to the door, and Reid gives his name and the bouncer lets us in. Xander is the last to walk in, looking like he'd rather be any place than here.

"Are you okay?" I ask him, slapping him on the back.

"Yeah, ummm…" He looks like he wants to say something to me, but we walk further into the strip club and the loud music cuts him off. A woman dances on stage, wearing nothing but those stickers that cover her nipples and a thong. I notice Reid not even looking her way as he orders drinks from a passing waitress. Why did he even want to come here? He doesn't care about any other woman besides Summer, and if he did, I'd punch him in the face. I have a feeling he's doing the big brother thing, him trying to let me experience everything, not wanting me to miss out on anything. Even something stupid as this. We're here just for the sake of being here.

We all sit at a table, Xander dragging his feet, the last to be seated. Tag stares at the stage, watching the woman dance for a second.

"Well, this is overrated," he says, and I burst out laughing. My thoughts exactly. I wonder what Taiya's doing, how their night is going. That's where I'd rather be, wherever she is.

"You're not going to make me get a lap dance are you?"

Reid laughs. "No, let's just have a few drinks and enjoy ourselves before we go home."

Sounds like a plan. We're talking about getting Dash a lap dance when something catches my eye. Not something, but someone.

My sister.

My fucking beautiful little baby sister.

She's wearing a tight top that shows off everything, and short shorts, standing by the stage, talking to another dancer. She walks past a table, and a guy grabs her arm and pulls her onto his lap.

I stand. Reid sees where I'm looking and stands up too, his face contorting in anger. Xander curses. Tag and Dash are staring in shock.

The man tries to kiss her, while she tries to squirm away.

I see red.

I stalk forward, ignoring Sephie's gasp when she sees me. Xander grabs her into his arms, taking her out of the way, and I punch the man right in the nose. Tag and Dash are holding Reid back, but just barely. A bouncer comes to grab me, and then Reid pushes Tag and Dash off him, and hits the bouncer in the jaw. A typical Reid Knox punch, the bouncer's head snaps to the side before he crumbles to the floor. More bouncers run up, four of them, and Tag and Dash face off with them. Reid grabs the second guy on Tag, while I take on the second on Dash. When they are all down on the floor, the four of us eye each other. I look around for Xander and Sephie, but it seems Xander took her out of the building, for which I'm grateful. Last thing I want is my little sister hurt in the crossfire.

I hear Reid curse and follow his line of sight, staring at the entrance where two police officers are walking in.

Fucking great.

And that's how we all spent the night in jail.

CHAPTER THIRTY

Taiya

I'm having the best night ever. Summer took us all to this male strip club, that's more like a show. We've been sitting at the table, drinking and catcalling all night. None of these men have anything on Ryan, but it has been a fun night out. I declined the offers for a private lap dance, instead content laughing with the girls. We're just leaving the strip club, ready for home when Summer gets a call from Xander. I hear her curse before she looks at me and cringes.

"What's wrong?" I ask her, instantly worried. Did something happen to Ryan?

"What is it?" Jade asks, stepping closer to Summer. Isis takes my arm, as if bracing for bad news.

"The guys got in a fight. They have to stay in jail overnight," she says, her eyes watering up.

"What the fuck," I growl, not expecting anything like this to happen.

Summer sighs. "Xander said they are fine, not to worry; they will explain everything. Then he tried to make light of it by reminding me about the first time we officially met."

"What happened?"

Summer cracks a smile. "I had to pick him up from jail. He spent the night in there for fighting. Xander's the only one not in jail this time because he had to look after Sephie."

"I thought Seph was at work?" I'm so confused right now.

"I'm sure there's an explanation. Let's just get home," Isis says, rubbing her arms for the cool breeze.

"Isis is right," Summer says. "Let's all go home. Do you guys want to stay at my place? Then we can go get the guys together in the morning."

"Sounds good," I tell her, grateful that I didn't have to spend the night alone worrying about Ryan. We call a taxi and wait for them to pick us up. We then head to Summer's. I try to go to sleep but all I can do is think about Ryan. What the hell happened tonight?

*****

Ryan's been home for an hour, and I'm still trying to process what he's just told me.

"So you went to a strip club, and Sephie works there? As a stripper?" My voice pitches higher with each word.

"Yeah," he says, his voice cracking a little. I look at the bruise on his cheek, the only evidence of him being involved in a fight. Sephie, a stripper? I really didn't see this one coming, that's for damn sure.

"Where is she now?" I ask him.

He swallows hard. "I haven't spoken to her yet." Poor Sephie, who knows what's going on in that head of hers right now. I cover my face with my hands, sliding them down and resting them on either side of my neck.

"Go talk to her, Ryan," I encourage him softly.

He sighs. "I know. I will. I just... come here," he says, opening his arms. I lean into him, closing my eyes, so happy he's back.

"I missed you last night," I whisper.

"I heard you had a sleep over. I'm guessing yours was better than ours," he says, startling a laugh out of me. "How was your night?"

"It was good, until my husband got arrested," I say as I trail my lips up his neck.

"I'm sorry, Tay. I just saw her there and lost my temper."

"I know." I reach my hand up and touch his bruise with my fingers. "Does it hurt?"

He grins. "No."

As if he would admit it if it did. "Are you too injured to make love to your wife?"

"Never, beautiful. Plus, I just got out of jail..."

I start cracking up laughing. "That one night in jail made you really horny, huh?"

"Well, I was hard all night picturing you in that school girl outfit, and what I was going to do to you, so yes."

"I can put it on again for you," I say, nibbling his ear lobe.

"Now?" he says, sounding extremely eager.

I decide to use this to my advantage. "No, not now. After you talk to Sephie."

He growls, "Are you bribing me, wife?"

"Yes, is it working?" I ask, batting my eyelashes. He stares at me with an intensity that makes me want to rip all my clothes off and beg for him to take me.

"I love you. You know that, right?" he says, his gaze holding mine.

My entire face softens as I look at him. "I know."

"You still love me, even if I'm an ex-con?" he jokes, hiding his smile in my hair.

"I'll always love you, no matter what," I say. "Even if you've done time."

He laughs. "You're amazing."

"I try," I say, my eyes still on his bruise.

He exhales. "I better go sort things out with my sister."

I inch away from him as he stands. "Be dressed in that uniform and waiting for me when I get home."

"And if I'm not?" I reply, lifting my chin up.

"Then you find out what happens to naughty girls," he says, his eyes sparking with mischief. He kisses my forehead. "Do you want me to bring you anything on my way home?"

I look down towards his lap.

Ryan laughs, "What am I going to do with you?"

"I have a few ideas."

"So do I," he says, kissing me before he walks out of the apartment.

Is it suddenly hot in here or what?

CHAPTER THIRTY ONE

Ryan

I don't think I'll ever understand women. I watch as Seph paces the small confines of her apartment. Throwing an evil glance at Reid and me every now and again.

"Why are you mad at us again? We just found out that you're a stripper and you've been lying to us about working in a café. I'm pretty sure it's us that should be pretty pissed off right now."

Reid grunts his agreement. Seph stops her pacing to glare at me. If looks could kill… let's just say, I'd be dead on the floor right now.

"You overbearing jerk! I'm not a stripper! I'm just a waitress there," she says, her chest heaving in anger.

I exhale in relief. Not an ideal job, but a million times better than a stripper. "It's not safe to work there. That man was putting his paws all over you," I say, trying to contain my anger.

"You're not working there anymore," Reid states, his tone deadly serious. Sephie gapes and I cringe. Way to go caveman.

"Well, you guys got me fired anyway," she says, flopping down opposite us on the couch. "I'm sorry I didn't tell you, but what was I meant to say? I've worked there for about two years now and I knew you wouldn't like it, or you would judge me for it, so I just kept it to myself."

"We just want you safe," Reid says, his tone now gentle.

"I get that," Sephie says, "but I really need the money. And no you two aren't helping me out financially."

"You would rather work in that sleazy bar instead of letting us help you?" I gape, my fists clenching. Stubborn infuriating woman.

She interrupts my mental rant. "If it's so sleazy, why were you even there," she says, back to scowling.

I pinch the bridge of my nose. "Work at our bar. We will pay you what you're getting now, or we'll double it. Whatever. How about that?"

She closes her eyes, thinking it over. "Fine."

I could jump for joy, but instead, I nod at her and try to school my expression. "What was with Xander?" I ask her, curious as hell about what's going on with them. Xander didn't want to go into that strip club, and I have a feeling he knew she worked there. No wonder the two of them have been all weird with each other. As if Xander would want his woman working in a place like that.

Sephie visibly flinches. "He somehow found out I worked here, told me to quit. I told him to leave me alone; he doesn't control my life. We weren't even dating... I mean... we were just starting to hang out together. I thought he would have told you. I was waiting for you to come and yell at me, but you didn't."

"Because Xander never told us anything," Reid says, looking over at me.

"He was just doing as I asked. Don't be mad at him," Sephie quickly says, standing up for Xander. Interesting. I want to be angry at him, but I can't. He wouldn't have betrayed her trust, and he's not the kind of guy to snitch.

"We aren't mad at Xander," I say, my eyes moving to the paintings on her walls.

"If it makes you feel better, he has a man follow me to and from the club to make sure I get home safe," she says, a smile playing on her lips.

"He does?" Reid asks, clearly shocked.

"Yes. I know we won't ever be together, but we do care about each other." She lays her head on one of her pillows. "I'm sorry you all got into a fight over it."

"Don't worry about it," Reid says. "As long as you're not working there anymore, I'm happy."

I stand. "I need to get home to my wife." I kiss Sephie on the head. "I love you, my stubborn girl," I whisper in her ear. "You coming with me, Reid, or you staying here for a while?" I ask him. We both rode our bikes here.

"I'll stay for a bit," he says. I wave bye and walk out, walking to get home to my woman.

We have unfinished business.

*****

When Reid calls me the next day with the news, I don't even know what to think or how to feel. This man wasn't a good person. In fact, prison was where he belonged, but now that he's dead, I don't feel any satisfaction. I guess dead or alive, there will always be a part of me that he's destroyed.

"How did he die?" Sephie asks boldly, a blank look on her face.

"Someone stabbed him," I mutter, looking down at my hands.

"Am I a bad person because I don't feel anything?" Sephie asks, looking out the window.

Taiya puts her arm around her. "You don't remember him, so no, it doesn't make you a bad person." Plus he was an asshole. Taiya is just too nice to bring that up right now. I wonder if Dad knew something was going to go down, that's why he told us about Sephie. I don't know if I'm trying to find good where there is none, but it's the only reason I can think of. Either way, all is well in the world. Sephie is safe with us and my father is… well, gone. To hell I assume.

Taiya watches me carefully, as if waiting for me to react. However, I don't think I have anything in me, other than a pang in my stomach, and a whole bunch of 'what ifs.' If only he could have been the father we needed, but he wasn't. And this is the end of that chapter. Reid and Summer come over, and we all hang out, order in Chinese and watch bad movies. We're just around each other, no words needed. We aren't exactly mourning, more like getting closure from a bad situation that has been a part of our lives since the day we were born. Since the day our mother was killed. I look around at the faces around me, and feel thankful. I look into Taiya's eyes and know this is exactly where I'm meant to be.

I'm one lucky son of a bitch.

EPILOGUE

Ryan

Having Xander and Seph in the same room is awkward as hell, well, at least for me. They keep eye fucking each other when the other isn't looking, and sneaking in longing glances whenever they can. I try my best to ignore them, instead concentrating on the celebration around me. Today is the official opening day for Taiya's dance studio. We decided to have a gathering here so everyone could check the place out. I started the party by getting into the middle of the dance floor and showing off my moves, which made Taiya burst out laughing. Don't think I'll be going professional any time soon, unless grinding my hips can get me qualified. It's just like sex, so I know I'm good at that. I hired a new guy to work at the bar, for events like this where everyone needs to be here. With Sephie working there now as well, I don't need to go in much, so I'm looking at other business opportunities to keep me busy. I've never been one to be idle. I need to be productive.

I see Taiya walk over to me, wearing a yellow sundress. She looks edible.

"Everyone loves it," she beams, pushing away an errant curl.

"It looks great. You did an amazing job. I'm proud of you," I tell her, pulling her close to my side.

"Me? This was all you," she says, going on her tiptoes to give me a kiss on the cheek. I want to ravish her right here and now, but that kiss is going to have to do until we get home.

"This is your dream, beautiful. Now you get to live it."

When I see her eyes starting to pool with tears, I flinch. "Don't cry."

"They are happy tears," she says, blinking furiously a few times. "And you're my dream, Ryan. This is just a bonus."

"You're so fucking sweet, Tay. Sweetest girl in the world. Happy tears or not, I still don't like seeing you cry," I tell her, playing with the thin strap of her dress. I kiss her on top of her head, and pull her to stand in front of me. I stare at the mirrored walls surrounding the entire wall, and instantly get ideas. All kinds of ideas.

"Ryan, why do you have your sex face on?" Taiya suddenly asks, interrupting my dirty thoughts and making me laugh.

"Sex face?" I have to hear this explanation.

"Yeah, you know, your bedroom face. Like this…" she says, giving me a smouldering look.

My laughter can't be contained. I can see the others staring at me like I'm crazy, so I just wave at them. Reid stalks over and gives me a weird look.

"Are you on something?" he asks me with a serious face.

I lean against the wall to steady me. "No. I'm just… happy."

Summer walks over and stands next to me. I wrap my arm around her. "Time for the after party?"

Summer looks at Taiya, "Can I take dance classes here?" she blurts out, looking excited.

"Of course you can," Taiya says. I see Reid eyeing the mirrors and start laughing again; his face takes on an intrigued look.

"I'm going to have to lock this place up, aren't I," Taiya mutters, shaking her head at us. Tag, Dash, Xander, Isis, Seph and Jade walk over, all smiles. They congratulate Taiya once more, and then we head to my apartment for the after party.

Life couldn't get more perfect.

*****

One week later

"You look so fucking beautiful," I whisper, staring down at Taiya. She's lying in the middle of the bed of our hotel room, dressed in her white gown, looking like a temptress slash virginal sacrifice. We just renewed our vows, and the day couldn't have been any more perfect.

"Are you going to stare at me all night?" she asks, sounding breathless.

"Amongst other things, yes."

Her pouty lips tug up into a smile. "I'm waiting," she says, lifting her arms above her head and thrusts her breast out. My mouth waters, wanting those sweet nipples in my mouth. I take my shirt off and throw it on the floor, followed by my pants and boxer shorts.

"I love you," I tell her, kissing her with everything I have.

235

"Show me," she replies, a challenge in her eyes.

I rip off her dress and do just that.

THE END

TOXIC GIRL

Coming April 2014

Everyone has secrets.

Finally, I had a fresh start.

I knew no one.

I could be anyone, or so I thought.

I wanted to be invisible, to blend into the background.

But it turned out keeping my secret wasn't as easy as I thought it would be.

Enter Grayson Mills.

When Grayson noticed me, so did everyone else.

He wanted me. Bad.

And what Grayson wanted, he usually got.

TIME
WILL
TELL

(Maybe, Book Three)
Coming 2014

Be spontaneous, they say.

That's how I ended up on the back of a stranger's bike.

A sexy, tall, tattooed stranger, but a stranger nonetheless.

How was I to know that a chance meeting with this man, Xander Kane, was going to change my life?

DESTROYED

by Pepper Winters

PREVIEW

COMING FEBRUARY 2014

BLURB:

She's a woman with a dirty secret.

I'm complicated. Not broken or ruined or running from a past I can't face. Just complicated. For good reason.

I thought my life couldn't get any more tangled in deceit and confusion. But I hadn't met him. I hadn't been sucked into his lies or taught to run from everything that he is. Instead, I let him ensnare me, seduce me, trap me with secrets—Hazel Hunter

He's a man with a killer secret.

I've never pretended to be good or deserving. Despite the shadows I live in, I'm ultimately a slave to my secrets and that gives me a free pass to chase who I want, be who I want, act how I want.

I didn't have time to lust after a woman I had no right to lust after. I told myself to shut up and stay hidden. But how could I deny her? How could I deny my one chance at redemption? But then she tried to run. I'd found a cure to my existence and damned if I would let her go—Roan Fox

And secrets silently destroy them.

First chapter subject to change, unedited, release date: 24th Feb.

PROLOGUE

Roan

I didn't believe her when she said she was complicated.

She didn't believe me when I said I had secrets.

I didn't understand the truth, even when she let me glimpse behind her mask.

She didn't understand that I couldn't live with the consequences.

I thought she was a saint.

She thought I was a sinner.

Too bad we didn't try to find the truth.

We both paid the price.

We destroyed each other.

ONE

Hazel

If I knew now what I suspected then, I'd like to think I would've done things differently. I would've planned better, worked harder, stressed out on more important things. But I was young, naïve, and woefully unprepared for the big scary world of life.

Now, I looked back on the past with a strange fondness. While I lived it, it seemed hard, but now it seemed so incredibly easy. Now, the present seems completely impossible and the future dire and bleak.

That is...until I met him.

Then it got worse.

*****

"I don't think this is a good idea, Clue." The gothic mansion rose from the gravel and soil like a beacon of doom. Gargoyles decorated plinths and overhangs; huge pillars soared to at least six stories high. I didn't know anything like this existed in Sydney, let alone in the rich and exclusive Eastern Suburbs.

Alarm bells hadn't stopped clanging in my head ever since we stepped off the train and headed toward a residential suburb instead of the party district in town.

Losing ourselves in a rabbit warren of streets, my heart never settled sensing this might be one experience that might end up killing us.

"Stop being such a worrier. You said you'd come. I need my wing woman," Clue said, her gentle voice turning slightly stern.

My mouth hung open, gawking at the intricate stonework, trying to see past the grandeur to reveal the tricks of such a place. It couldn't be real? Could it?

It seemed misplaced—as if it'd been transplanted from a long past century.

Huge double doors before us opened with a creak. Thick wood with wrought iron accents in the shape of a fox on a wintry night, revealed a black-suited bouncer with oil-slicked hair. His body looked like a mountain while his face looked like a cross between a bulldog and a biker.

But it was his eyes that froze me to the spot. He captured both of us with just one look.

"You better have the password; otherwise you'll wish you never set foot on this stoop." His gaze swept to the concrete stoop beneath us. A motto had been engraved painstakingly with a chisel. It looked hand done and rudimentary but held a certain threat all the same.

Was that Russian? I couldn't make out the verse, but I inched to the side in my stupid kitten heels to avoid standing in the groove of letters.

"We were invited by Corkscrew. He gave us a one night pass." For the millionth time since I'd showered, donned this ridiculous gold and silver dress and coaxed by thick chocolate hair into some resemblence of curls and waves, I wanted to throttle Clue.

She was my dearest friend, closest confident, flatmate, babysitter, and non-blood sister, but I wanted to kill her in that moment.

Clue and I had history. We were linked by shared dreams and hopes. We wouldn't let the other fail. And that was the only reason why I hadn't knocked her out and dragged her unconscious body back home.

She knew all I wanted to do was return to our crappy two bedroom apartment. She also knew I'd suffered so much in the past few weeks that I'd hit rock bottom and I had no energy left to fight. She'd taken advantage of my weakened state and in true friend fashion was sick of me moping. She wanted me to get up, bandage the road-rash, and keep going. Problem was, this time, I had nothing left.

Life had effectively pulled the rug, the flooring, and the fucking planet from under my feet. I didn't want to be here.

But as I grumbled and shed a tear or two on the couch, hugging my very reason for existence, she swore and cursed me.

She reminded me that I may be in a bad place, but she needed me. That life goes on, solutions come, and tragedies happen. I couldn't change the future either moping on the settee, or dressing up like a hooker and coming out with her.

So, as much as I wished I had a hacksaw in my cleavage so I could threaten her to take me home to Clara, I didn't.

"Corkscrew, huh? What discipline?" The bouncer crossed his arms, raking his eyes over me. I'd lost weight from the stress of the last few weeks, but I felt like a stuffed sausage in this slinky dress.

My stomach twisted as I plucked the loaned attire that clung to me like scales. A web of lace covered my shoulders, but it couldn't hide the sulttiness. My entire figure was on show, complete with perky nipples from the chill in the evening air.

Damn Clue and her fetishes for blingy, completely impractical clothing. I always seemed to be forced to wear the worst one.

She said I was too serious. Too focused. Too obsessed with creating a future where nothing bad from the past could find us.

And she was right.

Where she was a rainbow, I was the cloud. I never meant to turn into a weeping, rain-filled cloud. Life browbeat me into it until I gave up on colour and sacrificed happiness for survival.

Clara.

Tears pricked the back of my eyes again and I swallowed hard.

"Muay Thai," Clue answered, her black almond eyes flashing with pride. Her latest accusation, who I'd only met once, had successfully swept my commitment-phobic friend off her feet.

I didn't even know his real name. And Corkscrew, what the hell title was that?

"Ah, great sport." The bouncer relaxed a little, looking part gargoyle himself. "What's the password then, sugar tits?"

My mouth pursed. I couldn't stop the flash of fire; protective instincts rose to swell firmly in my chest. I'd always looked after everyone I came into contact with. I couldn't decide if it was a curse or a blessing to feel compassion and suffer such courage to defend another, but now the familiar fight built in me to protect Clue.

"Did you just call her *sugar* tits?" I'd never been one to stand by while another was ridiculed, embarrassed, or taken advantage of. I liked to think it was a strong character trait, but life had made it into yet another flaw.

He chuckled. "Well she has nice tits and she looks as sweet as sugar, so yeah. I did." His eyes narrowed. "You got a problem with that?"

Don't do it, Zel.

Clue patted my forearm and I forced the retaliation from my tongue. My hands clenched but I stayed silent. Giving him a verbal lashing wouldn't help us get into this illegal club for Clue to see her man candy.

Dismissing me, the bouncer looked back at Clue. "Spit out the code or leave. I don't have time for this."

Clue cocked her hip, accenting the fluidity of her amazing figure. Once again, I had a small flash of awe, taking in Clue's perfection. Dressed in an equally slutty dress she sparkled with red sequins. Looking part Geisha, part ninja warrior, Clue was one word: stunning.

She'd been the result of an illicit affair between a Chinese diplomat and a Thai prostitute. Born out of wedlock, she'd been thrown away like rubbish when she was just two weeks old.

We hadn't met until three years ago when I saved her from being raped and mutilated in a rural Sydney suburb. She knew my beginnings weren't as perfect as I told people, but she didn't know the whole truth either.

No one did.

"Thou may draw blood but never draw life," Clue whispered, layering her husky voice with a heavy dose of allure.

Even if the password had been completely wrong, the bouncer was so spellbound he would've let us in. Clue had magical powers over men.

"Well, what do you know? You're in." He swung the door wide, spilling warm light into the darkness of the night. "Head down to the end, then to the left. The main arena is there. Don't go into the other rooms unless invited."

Clue smiled and brushed past him, deliberately letting him gawk down her cleavage. "Thanks so much."

He nodded dumbly, letting me sneak past without fanfare.

My heart raced, taking in the ridiculous wide corridor. The heavy doors latched behind us and all I wanted to do was run home to her.

You left her alone. With strangers. For this.

For this? This decadence, this richness, this mockery of everything that I needed in order to save her life. Instead of tears, anger filled me.

Whoever owned this monstrosity had so much more than they deserved. If only life had been kind enough to give me a way out. Give me a way to save her.

"Clue. I've had enough. I'm sorry, but I'm leaving."

Clue spun again, grabbing my hands. "You're not, Zel. And I'll tell you why."

My temper rose further. It wasn't often that I got angry but when I did… not even an atomic bomb could match me.

Her thumb caressed my knuckles, trying to calm me but riling me up even more. "You're not going home. Mrs. Berry will take great care of her. You need to see that life hasn't ended outside our apartment. You need to remember why you fought so hard to get to where you are." Her voice softened. "I'm not only losing someone I care deeply for but my bestfriend, too. You can't die with her, Zelly. I won't let you."

The fucking tears that seemed to be a constant companion these days, shot up my spine in a tingling wake. I squeezed my eyes to stop them from spilling.

Clue gathered me into her arms, whispering in my ear. "You'll find a way. I swear. I know in my bones you'll save her. Just like you saved me. But you have to get out into the world to find a solution. You won't find it hidden in the cereal box in a dingy flat you haven't left in weeks."

I shoved her back. "I couldn't care less about the world. It took everything from me. And now it's taking Clara, too."

Clue tensed. "Remember who you are. You're a fighter. You didn't overcome your past to give up now."

"My daughter is dying and you think I'm giving up?" My voice wobbled and I stormed forward. I couldn't have this conversation anymore. Clue had valid points which just made me hate my self-pity and sadness all the more.

I couldn't rewind to the old Hazel. The twenty-four year old woman who'd been on the cusp of happiness. I'd had a great job—legal and law-abiding. I'd been healthy and content. And I'd had a daughter who I'd poured all my love and joy into; who made me a better human being.

You have *a daughter. Not past tense. Not yet.*

But Clue was right. I'd overcome so much already. I couldn't give up. I wouldn't lie down and let my daughter leave me—I had to find a cure and to do that I had to face the world and keep fighting till the end.

Bottling everything deep inside, I called over my shoulder. "You win, Clue. Let's go."

Her heels clicked on the stone work of the corridor, catching me up. Linking her fingers with mine, she murmured, "Tonight will give you the boost that you need. You'll see." Adding some bounce into her step, she added, "After all, we're going to watch men beat each other bloody. If that doesn't inspire you to get revenge and punch the world in its fucking face then I don't know what will."

I forced a small laugh, but she was right. In so many ways.

The corridor went on for ages, past huge swathes of material and massive nonsensical artwork of blizzards and forests, of darkness and wolfs, of a violent world. Sculptures made of bronze and iron guided us like centennials. A mix of modern art and intricate lifelike animals. All large, imposing, and entirely too real.

Grunting and panting came from behind one large door as we passed.

"I wonder what goes on in the private zones? More fighting, or do you think the victor steals a woman from the crowd and makes mad passionate love to her?" Clue's voice turned dreamy. "He'd be hot and sweaty and slippery with blood, but his kiss would make the girl forget. She'd let herself be consumed by the man who proved he was strong enough to protect her."

This time I laughed with my heart and not just out of requirement. "You're way too much of a romantic for these times, Clue. You should've been born six hundred years ago if you want men who kill and women who swoon."

She grinned, showing perfect pearly teeth. "I *was* born six hundred years ago. That's why I hanker after it so much."

I rolled my eyes. Clue had two fascinations in life: men and past lives. She swore she'd lived countless times before, and as much as I liked to joke and pluck holes in her tales, I couldn't ignore the fact that she knew things. Things she shouldn't know for a thrown away child with no education.

"You're an old soul too, Zel. I can tell. I haven't figured out where you're from, but I will."

I didn't have the heart to tell her she was wrong. I acted old beyond my years because I'd had enough bad fortune to last me forever.

I squeezed her hand as we turned left at the end of the corridor and promptly slammed to a halt. "Holy mother of God where have you brought me?" Dropping her fingers, I moved forward, almost in a trance.

The double doors had been crafted from metal. One side depicted a fairy-tale. A young man, with his face away from the viewer, stood surrounded by piles of coins, sunshine, and young children. Fantastical turrets of a castle rested in the distance.

My heart hurt as I looked at the next door. If the other had been heaven, this would be hell.

The young man now faced the doors but his features were blank. No nose or eyes or mouth, just a smooth oval. Behind him wolves fought while lightning and storm clouds brewed. But what killed me was the children who'd been laughing in the other portrait were now in pieces, scattered on the ground in melting snow.

"Whoa, that's a bit morbid," Clue said, reaching out to touch a severed leg.

I snatched her hand back and pressed the other door to open it. I wanted away from this scene. It came too close to home.

Don't think of your troubles. Tonight pretend to forget.

Troubles.

I could never forget about them. They were a noose around my neck. A guillotine waiting to fall.

The instant the door cracked open, noise assaulted us. A potent mix of fists hitting flesh, grunts of pain, lilts of feminine laughter, shouts of encouragement, and the smooth beats of music.

We entered a cavernous black room. Either a converted ballroom or a specially designed arena, it welcomed us with thick black velvet on the four story high walls. Lining the perimeter lived a grandstand sort of placement with black couches, la-Z-boys, and recliners. Each one had its own podium with side table and small lamp. Looking like fireflies in the dark.

"Oh, my," Clue murmured as we stopped scanning the side of the room and focused on the main event.

Every apparatus of fighting existed in this space. A Mixed Marital Arts Cage, a boxing ring, a Muay Thai ring, mats for close combat, and bare floor for other barbaric blood sports. Each space was crowded with men either bloodied from a fight or bouncing on their feet ready to meet a new opponent. Water stations and medic booths rested between each arena.

A huge banner hung from the ceiling directly above all five fighting rings.

Fight with honour, fight with discipline, fight with vengeance.

"I think I died and went to man heaven," Clue whispered, her almond eyes the widest I'd ever seen. Her cheeks flushed with colour as a man in the MMA cage took a hit to the jaw by a fighter glistening with sweat and blood.

The atmosphere in the room wasn't feral or violent, though. It had an old-world class about it. An exclusivity. A richness.

There were so many fighters I had no idea how Clue would find the man she'd come to see.

The music changed tracks from sultry to pulsing. Not so loud to distract the fighters, but it added yet another element to this strange illegal club.

Arms suddenly slinked around Clue, dislodging me from her side. I blinked as a tall man with cropped black hair and ebony skin gathered her close. "You remembered the address and password. I'm impressed." He nuzzled her throat, sending Clue into a flurry of lusty giggles.

My heart fluttered for her. I loved seeing her smile. I didn't think I'd seen her so infatuated before. My eyes flickered between the two. Where Clue was an Asian beauty, this man was an African Adonis. If they ever made it to procreation, their children would be spectacular.

The thought of children just sent me wheeling back to Clara. Her pretty, eight year old face filled my mind. Her long hair, so similar to my own, and her dark brown eyes, made my heart weep knowing our time together was running out.

She looked nothing like her father which I thanked the universe for every day. She was mine. All mine.

Not for much longer.

The memory shattered me and I stumbled a little.

Clue's man grabbed my forearm, steading me with a warm, strong grip. "You okay?"

Clue untangled herself from his embrace to support my other side. I felt like a waste of space, an invalid and an unfit human being. I needed to find my backbone again and stop wallowing in depression.

I couldn't ruin Clue's fun. I had no right. Not after everything.

"I'm fine. Sorry." Forcing life back into my voice, I asked, "So, you're Corkscrew?"

He laughed. "That's my fighting name, but yes. Tonight, I'm corkscrew." His dark eyes twinkled as he leaned closer. "My real name is Ben."

The normalcy of his name helped settle me a little and I smiled. "I like that. Two identities."

Just like me.

Up until recently, I'd had two personas. I'd spun tales and weaved stories as effortlessly as if it was the truth. It started as a game. An avenue to survive my past and paint a childhood I was proud of. To delete the wrongness and conjure an entirely new girl. I went from a gutter rat that bounced from foster home to foster home, never going to school, to a woman with style and poise. Someone with high school diplomas and career possibilities. I wrote my own story with a magical pen called lies.

And it worked.

I climbed from the mud and dreariness into sunlight and hope. I survived.

And now? Now, I was about to lose everything.

Clue interrupted my spiral into depression with a simple question, "What's this club called. I couldn't see any name on the building."

My interest spiked and my damn heart flurried. Something about this place gave me equal measures of unhappiness and hope. I hated the wealth dripping from every statue but at the same time never wanted to leave. I wanted to steal all the positive energy and strength that existed from the men and bottle it—create an elixir where my daughter would survive.

Ben smiled. "This is the best place on earth." Spanning his arms, taking in the club as if it was his own, he added, "Welcome to Obsidian."

ABOUT THE AUTHOR

New York Times & USA Today Bestselling Author Chantal Fernando is twenty six years old and lives in Western Australia.

When not reading, writing or daydreaming she can be found enjoying life with her three sons and family.

Chantal loves to hear from readers and can be found here:

https://www.facebook.com/authorchantalfernando

<3

Made in the USA
Middletown, DE
31 May 2023